Bad Move

Rydon Tyme: The Life of the Eye

Ali Muhammad

Bad Move is a fictitious story inspired by historic events, imaginative thoughts, and real life experiences of the author.

Published by Leaders of Tomorrow, Today LLC
PO Box 470 Oshtemo, MI 49077
First Edition

ISBN- 978-1-7356687-0-3

Front and Back Cover Illustrator: Aires Melo
Graphic Designer: LOTT Art Department
Story Illustrator: Aires Melo
Editor: M. Araujo

Dedication

This book is dedicated to the world. 2020 has been a very trying year. Between the pandemic and social struggles worldwide, it's clear to see that we have a long way to go. Reflect on your strengths and weaknesses. How can your strengths benefit us all? How can your weaknesses be strengthened? Plan, plot, and strategize. Your contribution to society might be the missing piece to the puzzle. We'll never know until you try.

I also dedicate this book to the city of Orangeburg, SC. This story was inspired by the Orangeburg Massacre of 1968. I researched the event after the deaths of Trayvon Martin, Eric Garner, and Mike Brown while writing this story in 2014. I didn't want to release it then. I didn't plan on releasing it now. Unfortunately, we're still facing the same problems that inspired the story six years ago. As a Writer, it is our responsibility to document the times.

Be sure to visit www.LOTT48203.com for books, blogs, careers, competitions, interviews, magazines, photo albums, press conferences, scholarship information, LOTT Sportswear, and more.

CONTENTS

Dedication i

Mackinac Island 1

Hampton, Virginia 10

Orangeburg, South Carolina 27

Columbia, South Carolina 34

Durham, North Carolina 35

Richland County Police Department 39

Chapel Hill, North Carolina 45

Macon, Georgia 54

Jacob City, Florida 60

Richland County Police Department II 64

Washington, D.C. 77

Preview: Prize Fighter 3 of 5

L.O.T.T.

Leaders Of Tomorrow, Today

"MAKE A SPLASH IN THE WORLD"

WWW.LOTT48203.COM

Skating amid a winter wonderland, courtesy of Mother Michigan, Rydon, and Gabriella Tyme were thoroughly enjoying their unexpected getaway. The couple created a separate bank account for emergencies and opportunities to finance what Rydon referred to as the E's and O's of life.

Zipping atop Lake Huron, the couple arrived at 8674 Haji Hill, a 942-foot, hilly terrain that towered over the lands of Mighty Michigan.

Rydon diversified himself throughout his forty-two years. He didn't restrict himself to stereotypes set by society. He did things that brought him happiness, willing to try almost anything once.

His wife, Gabriella, was the same, and together, they made the world their playground. Sitting on the edge of the frozen pier, Rydon removed the icy skates from Gabriella's toasty tots, briefly massaging and replacing them with snow boots.

"That feels so good. I promise, you read my mind," Gabriella giggled.

The two never lost lust for each other since the day they locked eyes. They were perfect for one another. Rydon Tyme was the most charming man she'd ever met, and fortunately for her, she was stuck with him for life.

He was her Prince Charming in the flesh, always leaving her blushing like a twenty-year-old. "Ry, how far did we just ice skate?" she asked with her head tilted back, resting on her heavily padded elbows.

"At least a mile, maybe two," Rydon replied.

The Tyme's were self-employed, adventurous, and loved to travel. They set their own office hours, essentially writing their own rules. The Mackinac Island getaway was much needed and appreciated.

"You want to warm up, or go snowboarding with me?"

Rydon enjoyed Haji Hill most; it was his favorite of all their getaways. In the summer, all of the action was on the east side of the hill, which featured a water slide leading right into Lake Huron. During the wintertime, the west side of the hill hosted many races down its snowy slope to the lodge at the bottom.

Long ago, the Tyme family built a house atop Haji Hill, overlooking the Lower Peninsula of Michigan. The cabin brought Rydon back to reality after his most mentally taxing cases in his second career as a public defender. His service to the community gave them high-quality representation at the expense of his emotional stability.

Rydon uncovered many ugly truths while working both jobs. The more he learned, the more disappointed he became. It was getting tougher by the day for Rydon to calm his nerves once his emotions got the best of him. Discipline and self-control suppressed his rage in the past, but in his forties, his patience wore thinner than the silver streaks on the chin of his goatee.

Lifting herself to her feet with the support of her husband's broad shoulders, Gabriella placed both hands on Rydon's frosty cheeks to kiss him goodbye. "Honey, I'm tired. I'm thinking, hot chocolate and a nap. I'll keep yours warm."

"Please do," he smiled, waving as he slid downhill.

Rydon had everything he ever wanted as a child, a beautifully decorated home, and fancy cars. He was wealthy and married to his soulmate, whom he loved whole-heartedly. Even still, something was missing.

Declining hundreds of feet in a matter of seconds, Rydon was finally at peace with his thoughts just days removed from closing his last case. Gliding, left, right, up, over, and higher, Rydon was effectively able to relieve stress with every leap and bound down Haji Hill.

Sliding to a stop, he grabbed hold to the tow rope, engineered by his great, great, great grandfather. On his way to the top, Rydon was immediately able to pinpoint the source of his disdain. He had grown up too quickly.

Everything he worked on had to be just right, even in grade school. He was a junior in high school when he saw his first B on an assignment.

In the same time span, he helped rewrite the record books during his high school's first state track and field finals appearance. All before adding college champion to his resume.

As a senior at California Midwest University, he ended his college career as valedictorian, graduating summa cum laude. Rydon Tyme was an old soul, a light-year ahead of himself, and it finally caught up to him.

Looking down on the state of Michigan from afar, he thought of all the things he missed out on because of how hard he worked. Arriving at the peak of Haji Hill, he knocked the snow from his boots and entered the family log cabin. Awaiting him with a look of concern, Gabriella stood ghostly, holding a cup of hot chocolate.

"You okay?" Rydon asked her.

"I think you should take this and have a seat," she answered, handing him a steaming cup of hot chocolate.

As her eyes burst into tears, Rydon's heart sank to the floor like a sack of silver. Never had he seen his wife so distraught. Holding her head against his chest, he waited for her to tell him what was going on

"Three students were shot," she sobbed.

"What?"

"Three kids died because," Gabriella sobbed, as she mumbled her speech.

"Gabby, what are you saying right now baby, speak English for me," Rydon pleaded.

"Chi just called. Three college kids were killed at South Carolina International."

"You have got to be kidding," he said, pulling one of the stools from underneath the kitchen counter. Rydon sat silently, shaking his head before pounding his hammer-like fist to the countertop in frustration. "I was just there last week!" he shouted, pushing the salt and pepper shakers across the countertop as they crashed to the oaken floor.

Rydon visited hundreds of colleges and universities, planting seeds of hope around the world, from the Atlantic to the Pacific. Six days earlier, he teamed up with one of the campus' student organizations to help incoming freshmen exercise their right to vote. The vibe he received from the campus reminded him of his undergraduate years in California.

The 1940s were some of his most carefree times. The Harlem Renaissance took place a couple decades prior, inspiring him to chase greatness. Artists he studied gave him enough motivation to last a lifetime.

Once a teenager blinded by the realities of the real world, rallying students against tuition increases were the only injustices he defended in those days. Years later, he grew into a highly recommended detective whose latest cases involved far too many fatalities.

The times changed tremendously throughout his career as a Private Investigator and part-time Public Defender. As a twenty-something, he brought justice to those who could barely make ends meet. In his thirties, Rydon fought for fair sentencing during nonviolent felonious cases.

Through his early forties, he found himself engulfed in the struggles of underrepresented American citizens who were still fighting for basic civil rights. Living in the same struggle as many of his clientele, he hated every ounce of it.

With every case Rydon took on, he resided amongst the population that hired him. Spending weeks and sometimes months with the castoffs of the free world—none lived his glamorous lifestyle. Most came from humble beginnings and still welcomed him to the neighborhood as if he were one of their own.

The people were quite fond of Rydon. He came in peace, seeking nothing but justice. "Everything was all good just a week ago, baby. I promise," Rydon said with his head hung.

"I already know what you're thinking. Don't burnout, Ry. You can't save everybody, all the time," Gabriella reminded him with a comforting back rub.

"I know. Gabby, believe me, I know."

"What are you going to do?"

"Call Chi. Did he leave a number?"

"I left it under the phone."

Embracing his wife in front of the stone fireplace, he knew what would happen next, and so did Gabriella. "Chi, how's it going, brother?"

"Rydon, I'm much better talking to you. It was horrific," Chi said slowly and somberly.

"What happened? Don't sugarcoat. The facts, Chi. I need facts," Rydon said sternly through the phone.

As an honest man, Rydon expected the same in return from any and everyone he dealt with. He needed to be able to trust the people around him, without a doubt. "After you left, the student body was ready for a revolution, right away."

"Really? I didn't think those college kids ever heard me when I talked," Rydon said, having a live flashback.

"You enlightened an arena full of folks, Rydon."

When speaking to students, Rydon never pulled any punches. He told them the one hundred percent, unfiltered truth about the real world, pros and cons. "That's deep," he replied.

—

4

"After you left, the College Union started meeting every night in the Fieldhouse, discussing student issues and concerns. They had so much success at the university level early on; they went straight to communities.

"Webster Akers and Redford Samuels were passing out fliers on the corner of Lancaster and Dorchester Street for a *Winter Peace Bonfire* they were having on campus. The boys approached a couple, inviting them to the event.

"Redford handed the man a flier. Instead of taking it and moving on with his day, he knocked the stack of papers out of Redford's hand and spat in his face. Told him to *stop stirring up trouble*."

"You're serious? How old was the couple?" Rydon asked.

"Forty sum'n," Chi quickly responded.

"I don't know what's wrong with our generation down south but too many of them are twisted in the head!" Rydon shouted into the receiver, losing his patience as Gabriella looked on from the living room. Curled in a ball with her back against the end of the love seat, she sobbed into the sleeve of her turtle neck.

"That's not even half of the story. Redford wiped the saliva from his face and slapped the man with his own saliva. The whole thing happened in all of five seconds."

"Wow," Rydon responded, as Chi's fingers snapped through the receiver.

"I grabbed the boys and got us out of there alive. Luckily neither of us was carrying, or it could've been worse. That was last Sunday, the fourth."

"All that hate happened over a Winter Peace Bonfire invitation?" Rydon asked. dumbfounded.

"Believe it or not," Chi answered.

"So, the boys were trying to make peace over what? The protests at the bowling alley?" Rydon asked, seeking more information.

"Yep, more and more folks started protesting. Next thing you know, things got violent and folks started getting thrown in the back of paddy wagons," Chi said.

"What happened to the world? Remember the 40s?" Rydon asked in a daze.

"Great times. Great times," Chi repeated.

"Then the Civil Rights War picked up dust in what, the mid-'50s? It hit me hardest after we lost Medgar and that was 62'. Seems like it's been downhill ever since. Sometimes, I wonder what would have happened if we went down south to counter-protest in those days.

"You know what I mean? Telling them to stick to themselves and build communities like ours up north. Instead of trying to go places where they weren't wanted.

"What sense does it make to say someone can't go somewhere because of their skin color? That's not logical thinking. I love what we accomplished. Some folks want to try other things and it's nothing wrong with that."

"I hear you, brother. We changed a lot of laws. Our best soldiers have been risking their lives for years in this war. It's just that Chi, a Civil Rights War."

During Homecoming Weekend of 1966, Rydon was invited to a rally hosted by the Black Tigers Security and Support System at his alma mater, California Midwest University. Motivated by the message, upon his return to the Great Lakes, Rydon founded Leaders of Tomorrow, Today.

LOTT was a security team and publishing house that safeguarded hundreds of neighborhoods throughout America. They communicated with citizens in their own newspaper. LOTT didn't work for city officials. They worked for the people and were sponsored by Right On Time Enterprises.

As an avid supporter of various social organizations, the Black Tigers Security and Support System inspired him most. They were all about bettering their communities. Citizen's arrest wasn't uncommon if one posed a threat to the public.

Their breakfast programs and crossing guards kept citizens safe and well fed. They paved the way for other security agencies across the United States, protecting communities from outside forces.

"You say that like you haven't been risking your life for years, fighting in the same war. You're one of the best Generals we have, Rydon."

"I appreciate that Chi," Rydon spoke calmly.

"Remember, I told you what I said wasn't even half the story?" Chi reminded him.

"Lay it on me," Rydon said, keeping an eye on his lady.

"He's one of us."

—

"He's a cop? If he's forty plus, he must have stripes, Chi. What kind of men do you have working under you?" Rydon questioned.

"He's a Sergeant but not from my precinct. I never knew the man existed before last Sunday," Chi said, tapping a pen on his desk.

"It's bad this doesn't surprise me. Guys like them seem to spread like wildfire, Chi," Rydon replied, swiping at the dishrag sitting on the counter.

"That's why I called you. We're going to nip this in the bud and bring you in, undercover," Chi assured him. "They won't even see it coming."

"What else happened, Chi? I need the whole story."

"The man picked up one of the fliers… folks said he harassed the boys on campus every day since. This last Wednesday, the boys went to the store before class and Officer Scott cited them for jaywalking."

"Jaywalking? Three kids died for organizing and jaywalking? Is that what I'm hearing!?" Holding the phone away from his mouth, Rydon let out a huge sigh after yelling into the receiver. Looking over to Gabriela whom he heard crying, Rydon was at a loss for words.

"I know, brother, it makes no sense. Witnesses say they threw the boys against a fence and jammed them up. The boys fought back, and that's when Sergeant Lynch roughed them both up.

"The next night, Sergeant Lynch and Officer Scott showed up at the bonfire," Chi paused. "And put the fire out."

"Was it rowdy?" Rydon asked.

"Doesn't seem like it. They partnered with some of the frats, sororities, and other organizations to help out. Sounds like it was a night full of activities that ended with the bonfire. They had it set up real nice. A photographer and filming crew worked the event. They don't have much footage after the shootings started. Kinda bittersweet when you think about it," Chi spoke with empathy.

"So, why'd they say they put out the fire?" Rydon continued to question.

"Fire hazard's the claim. Hard to back that up when tickets are needed to get in. The university tracks attendance at all campus events."

"Sad, Chi, sad," Rydon said full of glum.

"Some students said they screamed and called them names for putting out the fire. A few folks saw bottles thrown at the squad car. Staff members said it was uncalled for and that made the students react. That's what we're hearing happened before Lynch and Scott fired into the crowd.

—

7

"That's all we know right now, Sergeant Lynch and Office Scott emptied their magazines into a crowd of over two hundred folks. Twenty-eight people were wounded, three fatalities. Two seemed to be targeted and a stray hit another student, Chad Jefferson III. They were all seniors.

"Lynch and his partner say fire logs were thrown at them. We talked to the students. We talked to staff. No one saw any fire logs being thrown, but they all saw and or heard shots being fired into the crowd. We searched the scene, didn't find any burned logs outside of the fire pit. However, we did find what looked like the banister of a porch on the scene.

"Right now, it's unclear if it was thrown at the officers and If so, was it before or after the shots were fired. The other side to it was that it could've been used for cover. It was big. We're pretty sure it came from an abandoned home across the street." Chi concluded, causing a gap in the conversation.

"Nope. No way this happened in real life," Rydon intercepted, in pure disbelief. "I can't deal with this right now. I'm on the hill with the wife. I just wrapped up a case three days ago, I'm tired, Chi.

"I feel responsible for all this, rallying those kids like that," Rydon paused. "I'll send Virginia LOTT over to help with the riots and I'll be down early next week," Rydon said

"Thank you, Rydon! We appreciate it, brother, really. I owe you one," Chi said gratefully.

"I'm going to hold you to that. Chi, I have to go. Peace."

"Rydon?" Chi called out.

"I'm here," he replied.

"Don't have ill will for inspiring folks. Stay safe, brother."

"Thanks, brother, you too. I'll keep that in mind. Peace."

Under normal circumstances, Rydon took on no more than four to six cases per year. On average, he solved his cases in less than four weeks. However long it took to close a case, he vacationed for the same length.

His last case was three months and three days later, he found himself agreeing to join a corrupted police force and establish *True Blue*.

"I'm not sure how much longer I can do this, baby. I feel like everything I do is undone five times faster than it took to accomplish in the first place."

"I've been telling you that since we were in our twenties, Ry. You work too hard," Gabriella shrugged.

—

"If I don't, who will Gabby? Some of my allies are my enemies right now."

"I know, Ry. You want me to come down south with you this time?" she comforted.

"I don't want the police force to see you and think I'm with you. I have to go undercover for this one."

"Be careful baby, things are a lot different down south," Gabriella reminded him.

"You don't ever have to worry about me, sweetie. I will always be alright," Rydon assured her, kissing her temple.

"You always say that."

"Have I been wrong yet?" he wondered.

"Nope."

Hampton, Virginia

Interstate 95, South

8:05 a.m. Eastern Standard Time

1968 February 12, Monday

"I'm driving down instead, Chi. I'm in Virginia now. I need some inspiration for this one. I'll be here a few days, and I'll see you Friday morning."

Many of Rydon's childhood heroes helped shape history in the state of Virginia. After the Civil War, seventeen states led the way: Alabama, Arkansas, Delaware, Florida, Georgia, Kentucky, Louisiana, Maryland, Mississippi, Missouri, New Jersey, New York, North Carolina, South Carolina, Tennessee, Texas, and Virginia. As agreed upon after the war, politicians representing the former Confederacy and Border States allied with Civil Rights Activists to reshape the community.

Just over one hundred years later, LOTT partnered with organizations to help bring peace to the streets in each of the seventeen states. Year after year, Freedom Hunters, slave descendants, political prisoners, and revolutionaries of the past stepped up to the plate so history would not repeat itself.

"No problem, Rydon. Take your time. Things won't be changing here anytime soon," Chi sighed.

Arriving at the Douglass University training facilities, Rydon was greeted by a familiar face who reminded him of himself years earlier. He was young, self-motivated, and full of brilliant ideas.

"Dr. Tyme, how are you, sir? Long time no see," the young man said, catching up to Rydon's pace.

"What's up, big fella? How's the season going?" Rydon asked, shaking his hand.

"We don't mess around, Doc. We're undefeated, twenty-five wins, no losses," he replied, waving his hand to ease the pain while Rydon looked away.

"Good to hear. That's one of the reasons I'm here, to check out the team. I need a getaway before my next case."

"You headed to the Carolinas?"

"What makes you ask that?" Rydon wondered.

10

"Everybody's headed that way, Doc. Pro athletes and entertainers. The Superior Seventeen landed a news chopper on the fifty-yard line. They brought a team of reporters with them too, I hear," the young man said, spreading the word.

Rydon went on to become a megastar, by mistake. Although he wore no mask, he always managed to go unrecognized to the public eye. The Superior Seventeen was the exact opposite. They not only embraced their newfound stardom, they created it.

The Superior Seventeen were Rydon's alter egos. Flashy, arrogant, and unpredictable but above all, they found answers and got things done. They were the charter members of LOTT and were responsible for training its security teams. His first students didn't stop there. They founded Real Newz and took them wherever they went.

"Double $ is headed down south with The Newz Team? That's what I'm talking about!" Rydon shouted, pumping his fist.

"Yes, sir! We almost went too but coach said it wouldn't be right, not to play for our school. Coach convinced Dean Shaw to let us take the buses to Orangeburg after our game, so it's a win-win situation."

"That's righteous. I'm proud of you boys standing up for what you believe in. Where's Coach? I was looking for him, not you scrub," Rydon joked, playfully punching the young man's arm.

"I average fifteen points, eleven assists, and seven rebounds on an undefeated team. You know I'm great. We're coming for Cal Midwest's hundred-yard relay record in the spring too by the way. Book it, Doc!" he snapped back, rubbing his arm while Rydon searched for Coach.

"Man please, that record is older than you are. However, I wish you the best of luck. I'm going to let you get to class, superstar. I'll see you later," Rydon replied, pounding fists with the young man. "Stay great."

After receiving his post-graduate degrees in Journalism and Law from Michigan International University, Rydon headed south for his doctoral program.

An extended break from the classroom prompted his return with a vengeance, graduating with honors as Dr. Rydon Tyme from Douglass University in Hampton, Virginia. His most recent title as a psychologist, made him sound older than he felt at forty-two.

"Coach, how are you?"

"Rydon, my man, what's going on?" he replied with a man hug.

"You know me, getting ready for the Carolina's," Rydon shrugged.

"We're going down after the game. Are you staying for it?"

"B Hamp was just telling me about that. When is tipoff?" Rydon wondered.

"Thursday at 8."

"Perfect, I'll hit the road with you all. I need to talk to Cato. Have you seen him yet? I heard they touch downed on the fifty-yard line. I love them, man, I really do," Rydon asked, playing catch with a basketball he found along the way.

"He told me, *somebody had to*; when he came by earlier. He said you'd know where to find him."

Junior Cato was the leader of Virginia LOTT. Rydon was introduced to Cato at a peace rally on the west coast in 1944. Cato was only twelve at the time. As Virginia LOTT's Leader, Junior Cato and his security team helped cut the city's major crimes in half after his first quarter at the helm.

He found success early on by going into the neighborhoods, directly to the source of the problem. After a thorough rehabilitation process, he hired former misfits to protect the communities they once destroyed. Cato's street smarts allowed him to represent tens of thousands statewide.

Arriving at Miracle's Books and Copies, Rydon placed his heavy hands on the shoulders of his protégée.

"You almost scared me but I already saw you walk in through my dreams, brother. Nice try," Cato replied, lifting the bucket hat that covered his eyes.

"Same ole Cato. How are you, sir?" Rydon laughed, shaking hands.

"I'm living, so I'm satisfied for now. Enough about me, I hear you go by Dr. Tyme now. Congratulations, Doc!" Cato shouted in an empty corner aisle.

Often wrapped up in the needs of the world, Rydon rarely enjoyed his own accomplishments. It seemed as if others were more proud of him than he was of himself. "Thank you, I appreciate it. I thought you were in Orangeburg? B Hamp said you all landed on the fifty-yard line."

"You heard about that?" Cato asked.

"I loved it!"

During his days mentoring the Superior Seventeen, Rydon was a strict disciplinarian. After they matured, he let them live their own lives, free of scorn. They were no longer his students but allies in the war for liberty. He understood the power of their voices and together they were the leaders of the new school.

"I never know how to read you, Doc. I try to wait before I say too much. You still make me think you're going to make me do pushups or run a mile. We flew here when we heard you were coming to town. You know Chi can't keep his mouth shut," Cato laughed.

"It's not on The Newz is it?"

"No, sir. We know you too well. No video footage until after you split. We always got your back. Everybody knows you're headed down South by the way. You were Chi's recruiting tool."

"I figured. They have to find me to see me and they won't find me," Rydon said, slapping Cato on the shoulder.

Rydon was allergic to fame. He despised it greatly. As a boy wonder, no one outside his close circle of friends and community members knew he existed. Over the last decade, everyone knew his name and expected the world from him all of a sudden.

His problem with the spotlight wasn't being treated like royalty. It was seeing people who looked like him be treated like scum. Rydon was a package deal. You couldn't get him without the people.

—

13

Hampton, Virginia

Douglass University Fieldhouse

7:22 p.m. Eastern Standard Time

1968 February 15, Thursday

"Dr. Tyme! I'm glad we caught you," a student shouted from afar, gaining Rydon's attention.

"Yes, you did, but how? You all are slicker than I," Rydon questioned.

"Coach had us on lookout. He said you might try to sneak in."

"He was absolutely right," Rydon confirmed.

"Why don't you like people, Dr. Tyme?" the young man wondered.

"I love the people. What do you mean?" he asked, shocked by the question.

"You always seem like you're hiding when you come here."

"I am always hiding. If people know I'm in town, I can't do my job. As long as I stay discreet, the bad guys will keep acting up. That's when I come in and catch them red-handed."

"That makes sense," The young man said mid-thought.

"I thought so too. Now tell me this, why does coach have you all stalking me?" Rydon asked, seeking answers.

"He wants you to judge the Slam Dunk Tournament," the young man said, laughing.

"Go tell coach I wouldn't judge if the job paid in silver and gold. After that, tell him I'd love to."

Recreational activities always excited Rydon. They were his outlet. Too often, he got lost in the lives of others; he rarely enjoyed his own.

Walking across the glossed, hardwood basketball court, Rydon admired the banners and retired jerseys hanging from the rafters.

The energy never seemed to leave the gymnasium. It always felt like a big moment was seconds away. "Coach, your spies crept up on me like a thief in the night. Do you have them on payroll?" Rydon asked, knocking on the door as he entered Coach Grand's office.

"I'm glad they caught you. What do you think?" Coach Grand laughed.

"As long as I can get the first dunk of the night, I'm in," Rydon agreed with a handshake.

"Can those rusty knees still bounce like they used to? It's a lot of cameras out there," Coach Grand reminded him.

"Rusty? I stretch daily and that's before my morning miles, with an *s*, Coach. You of all people should know my golden knees don't tarnish."

"Remember the way I leapt pass you on the scoreboard when we high jumped in undergrad? I'm going to do the same but wave as I fly tonight," Rydon said, predicting the future.

"You probably haven't played ball since you finessed the commission out of a year of eligibility at MIU," Coach Grand said, laughing out loud.

"I didn't finesse anyone out of anything," Rydon chuckled. "I only ran track for three years at Cal Midwest. It's not my fault I graduated early," he shrugged.

It was no doubt where the Superior Seventeen learned to trash talk. In private, Rydon was as real as they came. To the public eye, he was a complete mystery. He never took an interview unless it was for Real Newz Network and gave little to no respect to the paparazzi who made a living invading his privacy.

"Whatever old man, that was before you hit forty. We'll see what you got in about fifteen minutes. I'll match your opening dunk with a three ball after we close them out."

Minutes before tipoff, Coach Grand allowed Rydon to deliver the pregame speech to the undefeated Douglass University Outlaws.

"Raise your hand if you've ever missed a shot during warmups. Keep them up. Put your other hand in the air if you've ever missed a layup. Look around, none of us are perfect. We already know that, but they don't. You're undefeated. They don't know anything about you all except what you show them. As far as they know, you all are perfect until you prove them wrong.

"Three college kids your age will never hear about what you all are getting ready to do tonight. Tonight, you men are going to play unselfish, high speed, physical, Outlaw Basketball. Drop your hands and say *Uh oh.*"

"Uh Oh!"

"Hands in, hands in, hands in. *Bad move* on three, 1! 2! 3!"

"Bad move!"

The booming voices of the Douglass University Men's Basketball Team echoed around the arena. Looks of doubt smeared across the faces of The Columbus University Renegades.

"Fellas one more thing," Rydon said to the team. "Do you all still do tip drills off the backboard?"

"Yes sir! At the end of every practice," Bobby barked back, full of adrenaline.

"Ok let's run the course, I'll bring up the rear."

Senior redshirt point guard, Bobby Hampton, took off in a sprint towards the rim with a sea of blue trailing behind him. He tossed the basketball off the backboard with finesse. Eleven other teammates followed, catching the ball, bouncing it off the backboard to the teammate behind them.

Frank Tyson, a four-time All-Nation center ended the constant flow of Outlaws, bouncing it once more off the right side of the backboard. As it ricocheted off the glass, the ball landed perfectly into the palm of six-foot Rydon Tyme.

Placing the ball behind his back, Rydon dunked it with a graceful left-hand finish. The loudspeaker blared, reintroducing the living legend to the erupted crowd.

"Doctor Rydon Tyme and your Douglass University Outlaws. Ladies, gentlemen, boys, girls, women, and babies, show your love!"

The stadium roared like an African safari. His return to the city that taught him how to be a man was one for the ages. Some of his most notable cases came during his doctorate studies.

Never skipping a beat, it was business as usual. Looking over to the Columbus Renegades sideline, whose players admired their opponents. Rydon gave the head coach a fierce look, before wiping the sweat from his forehead.

Raleigh, North Carolina

I-95 South

3:16 a.m. Eastern Standard Time

1968 February 16, Friday

On a crowded bus full of excited athletes, coaches, students, and revolutionaries, Rydon stood at the front ready to make a statement.

"Can I have everyone's attention for a moment. Great game to the men's basketball team. They made it look easy out there. I knew you all were undefeated, but did you have to beat them by twenty-seven? I guess so," he shrugged. "Great game fellas. Coach and I thought you all might need a break before we get to Orangeburg, so we planned a little detour.

"A wise woman once told me, the only place success comes before work is in the dictionary. She was absolutely right. What you all are about to witness in Orangeburg will shake many of you to the core. It will be a life-changing experience, I can guarantee it. For now, just enjoy the scenery and deal with Orangeburg when we get there.

"We'll be there soon, and please don't ask any questions about where we're going or how long it'll take. Life is a journey, enjoy it and try to get some sleep. It's four in the morning. I love you all. Goodnight!"

Anticipation filled the bus as the team sent a thank you to Dr. Tyme and Coach Grand.

Myrtle Beach, South Carolina

7:07 a.m. Eastern Standard Time

1968 February 16, Friday

Rydon led the undergraduates, faculty, and staff to the best seats on the beach. It was enough space for every past time one could imagine.

"To my fellow grillers, we're going to set up over by the gazebo. They have basketball and volleyball courts over by the parking lot. After we finish eating, I'll help lead my team to the inaugural, Myrtle Beach Bowl Two on Two Tournament. Coach, show them the trophy," Rydon said, motioning to Coach Grand with his spatula.

Coach Grand held a silver football-shaped trophy high in the sky as the sun reflected sharply to the pupils of those watching in awe. With the beach party in full motion, students became more outspoken.

"Doc, it's time to go," Cato said, taking Rydon's cooking utensils.

"What are you talking about, Cato?"

"You are being relieved of your duties. It's time to have some fun. Drop the tongs, or Virginia LOTT will be forced to thrash you," Cato said, holding a large sack of water balloons.

"I'm scared of you, young buck. I give up! B Hamp, don't burn those burgers. Not too much sugar in that lemonade, Frank. Be careful how much salt…"

Rydon's biggest problem was that he was imprisoned by his own happiness. He saw the world for what it could be, and it became his driving force. Rydon liked things his way, which meant he had to do it himself most the time.

"Doc, why do you work so hard?" Cato asked.

"I don't have a choice. If I don't do it, chances are it won't get done."

"I disagree, Doc. You have thousands ready to take orders on command. Everyone is waiting on a chance to impress you, but haven't received the opportunity."

"What are you talking about, brother?" Rydon asked, genuinely confused.

"Chi assembled us all last week. He said you were the only person who could bring justice to Orangeburg."

"Chi said that?"

———

19

"He said a whole lot more, Doc. He recruited over two thousand people who are waiting on your orders. Another thousand are expected over the next couple days," Cato informed him.

"Chi made it seem like this was a low-profile job. Thanks for the heads up, little brother. I'm going to need a ride to the airport for a car after this, and I'll meet you all there," Rydon said, making an audible.

"No problem, Boss. Let's go dunk some folks in the water. It's too much dry skin on this beach."

Always the life of the party, Rydon Tyme and Junior Cato woke up the sandy sleepers. Three buses of support from the Old Dominion crowded the beach and Rydon could only marvel at his present sights.

"The coin toss is in ten minutes, you ready, Doc?" Bobby asked, throwing Rydon a tight spiral.

"Is water wet? Of course, I'm ready. Are you playing with the champs tonight or do you plan on losing?"

"Whoever picks me are the real champs," Bobby preached.

"Well, B Hamp, you know how much I like going up for the jump ball. If you don't get picked first, we'll make them regret it."

"Sounds like a plan," Bobby said, pounding fist.

With the game tied at forty-two, it came down to the last play of the regulation to determine a winner. Bobby dropped back to throw the ball just as Rydon blew past Coach Grand.

Sensing the mismatch at the pre-snap, the point guard turned quarterback already had things planned. Rolling out of the pocket bought him enough time to spot Rydon running full stride towards the end zone as he threw the ball up for grabs.

Leaping into the air, Rydon caught the ball over two defenders as they crashed to the sand. The beach erupted like an overtime thriller, carrying the Myrtle Beach Bowl champions all the way back to the bus.

Myrtle Beach, South Carolina

Myrtle Beach City Airport

3:03 p.m. Eastern Standard Time

1968 February 16, Friday

After celebrating in fashion on the team's luxurious charter busses, the group of scholars made a pit stop at the Myrtle Beach City Airport. Waving farewell to his allies, Rydon walked into the facility to rent a vehicle for the case.

Reaching the counter, he was greeted by a chipper receptionist. "Hello there, sir, I hope your day is going well on this fantastic Friday."

"My day has been fantastic actually, thanks for asking. I hope the same to you. Check this out. I need a sturdy truck, preferably by Pentagon Motor Company. They just released a four-door truck, the Stallion, I think it's called. Do you all have any of those in stock?"

"Yes, it's actually called the Pentagon Passion. It's a four-door truck with an accessible hatchback. It has a sleek, steel frame with a silver emblem on the hood.

"We have four in stock. Black, metallic silver, midnight blue, and forest green. We also have the upgraded version with the same engine used in the Pentagon Sledge Hammer. You will be the first to drive the vehicle. We just purchased them last week."

"Nice, I'll take the upgrade in midnight blue. You're really good at what you do. I don't know if anyone has ever told you that before," Rydon praised the receptionist.

"I hear it all the time and it's people like you that make it easy for me to get out of bed every day. Thank you, Dr. Tyme. Here's your license. Our waiting area is just over here to your left and my right. I hope you enjoy your ride."

"Thank you. I'm sure I will."

Reaching the driver's seat of his new loaner vehicle, Rydon coasted south on U.S. Route Seventeen.

Charleston, South Carolina

The Airport of Charleston, West Terminal

5:09 p.m. Eastern Standard Time

1968 February 16, Friday

Grooving to the melodies of The Desires, Rydon was lost in the soul music blaring from his speaker system. Merging onto Interstate twenty-six, he finally reached his destination. Arriving at the west terminal, he parked in the twenty-minute parking lot.

Unsure of what to expect next, he walked over to the Destiny Air Crew terminal of the airport. Waiting for passengers to exit the plane, he could only hope his sidekick got the message.

Taking a seat in the lobby, Rydon felt the weight of the world on his shoulders. For the first time, he felt bigger than life itself. Born in 1925, in Highland Park, Michigan, Rydon was educated by one of the top ten school districts in the United States. Growing up in what seemed like a perfect world.

As of late, however, the world he lived in had been tainted by power. Rydon was a giver who was trapped, roaming in the lands of takers. Feeling like a loner, he was on the brink of a breakdown when two warm hands covered his fiery eyes.

"Guess who?"

"You got my message. Baby, I'm so happy to see you," Ryon said, squeezing her.

Gabriella Tyme dropped the hyphen on Rydon's fortieth birthday. Even though he never asked her to, it was her way of showing him that she was committed to him and their marriage one hundred eleven percent.

After a conversation on the beach, Rydon slipped away to make a call, inviting his wife to work with him during his next case. Unfortunately, she wasn't home. His wish was then placed in a message he left with the sheriff of a nearby county. Miles away from the family's Upper Peninsula log cabin.

"Do I smell like cake? I've never seen you like this before," Gabriella blushed.

"Is it a crime to show the woman I love how much I missed her? You keep me sane through all of this nonsense," he reminded her, hugging tightly.

"I like the way you say that. Say it again."

"I missed you," he said, kissing her cheek. "Especially since we weren't together Wednesday," Rydon said with a sigh.

"We celebrated early, Ry. It's OK," she said, kissing his bearded cheek in return. "And I missed you too."

As the lovebirds embraced each other, strolling down the hallways of the west terminal, Rydon briefed his wife on the most current events. "Two thousand people, Ry? Are you serious?" Gabriella said, eating a basket of fries from the airport food court.

"I said the same thing. I thought I was overreacting," Rydon said with relief.

"That's a lot of people, what are you going to do?"

"Chi told me I'd be undercover so I expect him to keep his word. Unless, *bring you in, undercover,* means something else these days," Rydon said, shaking his head. "I'll ride in sometime tonight."

"I'm surprised you let me come; you never let me come with you," she said, sipping ice cold lemon water from her straw.

"You still can't. You're staying right here in Charleston. There's a Black House Suites not too far from here. We can get you a room right now."

"That works too. I hear they have hot tubs and spa services in the penthouses."

"Penthouse?"

"I'm your guest Ry, you're kind of obligated to show me a good time."

"This is going to get expensive, I can see it now," Rydon said, shaking his head.

Opening the door to the top floor, the couple eased into Gabriella's penthouse suite.

"I won't be able to see you freely. We'll have to meet up at specific times and places. I don't want anybody to know that you're here."

Rydon jotted down locations on a notepad where the two would meet each weekend. "Durham, Chapel Hill, Macon, Jacob City, Columbia. Ry, only one of these places are in South Carolina. How am I going to get around?"

"Airport shuttles, taxis, either or," he said capping his ink pen.

"If I'm in a different city every week and there are five cities on the list, you're expecting to be here five weeks?"

"At least; it could be longer," Rydon reasoned.

"About that taxi," Gabriella said, negotiating the terms. "I was thinking matching Pentagons. I'll take a Pink Fantasy?"

"Absolutely not, you're supposed to be discreet. I agree, you do need to get around but you have to blend in. Fantasies are too flashy. You need something blue-collar, like a Pentagon Panther, a sturdy, reliable, good looking car. You have a Fantasy at home anyway," Rydon countered.

"I have a purple Fantasy; I want pink. Panthers are fine too, I suppose. I'm getting kind of excited going to all these places but I do have a question?"

"I'm all ears," Rydon said, listening attentively.

"If this is the only time we'll see each other in South Carolina, can I go back to Michigan and fly from home?"

"How many times have you asked to work a case with me over the last twenty-plus years?"

"Easily a million," she guessed.

"How many times have I said no?"

"One million one. I didn't even bother to ask this time. I already knew your answer," Gabriella giggled.

"Do you want the job?" Rydon offered.

"What job?"

"Living in those cities on the list for a week. You won't be in fancy suites though. You'll be living with family and extended families that I trust. They'll have their boots on the grounds so make sure you wear comfortable shoes. We'll meet on Fridays and Saturdays. I negotiated weekends off with Chi.

"On Sunday afternoons, you'll be on to the next city, and I'll be on my way back to South Carolina. We'll start tomorrow in Durham and then next week, Chapel Hill.

"The good thing about it all is if we get spotted, it will look like we're vacationing instead of working. Your main responsibility will be talking to the people of the neighborhood about what's going on in Orangeburg. After we bring peace to Orangeburg, it's off to Washington D.C. to present our findings to the people. All the little girls are going to want to be like you when they grow up."

"You're serious about this?" Gabriella hoped.

"Is macaroni cheesy? Of course, I'm serious. Do you want the job or not?" he laughed.

"I'm speechless. Ry, I'd be honored. I feel so important."

"You are important."

Orangeburg, South Carolina

Western Shore, Lake Marion

6:03 pm Eastern Standard Time

1968 February 16, Friday

Finally reaching his destination hours behind schedule, Rydon was back to the drawing board. He despised the media and the attention they brought with them because he saw himself as a regular everyday citizen of the world.

He didn't consider himself an idol and didn't feel better than anyone else to deserve the unwanted attention. Rydon couldn't conceptualize why he was so sought after for interviews and cameo appearances out of nowhere.

Over the last twenty-six years of his career, much of his work had gone unnoticed to the public eye. He was able to fly under the radar until taking a phone call while on vacation at a Windsor hotel resort on the last day of 1958.

It was a phone call he slightly regretted taking, a call that catapulted him to superstardom where he remained ever since.

Slowly pulling into the hotel parking lot, Rydon turned off his radio, resting in the deafening sound of silence. Feeling defeated for the moment, he thought ahead to the events in Orangeburg and sulked in the driver's seat.

Unpacking his bags from the oversized trunk of the Pentagon Passion, Rydon strolled through the revolving doors of the Heavenly Peace Hotel and Suites just off the shore of Lake Marion.

A man dressed in an all-white uniform took his bags the minute he entered the lobby. Usually, Rydon rejected the helping hand but at that moment, he needed all the assistance he could get.

"Greetings, sir. Welcome to Heavenly Peace Hotel and Suites. How may I assist you today?"

"Hi, I just need a room for tonight and a calling card if you have any," Rydon requested, reaching for his wallet.

"Sure thing, I'll just need your driver's license or identification card."

Arriving on the fourth floor, Rydon walked the halls searching for his room. Turning the key to room 463, he entered with a sigh of relief. His view of Lake Marion was second to none. The fountain in the center of the lake provided peace as promised in the hotel's name.

Rydon toured the suite finding the bathroom most attractive. Marble floors, a walk-in shower, wall-to-wall mirrors, and the Jacuzzi in the corner quickly caught his eye like silver in the sun.

After mentally preparing for his latest assignment, Rydon knew it was time to take care of business.

"Orangeburg Police Department, this is Toni speaking. How may I help you?"

"How are you, Toni? Is Major Chi available?"

"Yes, sir. May I ask whose calling?"

"No, thank you. He'll know who I am," Rydon rejected sternly.

"One moment please."

Waiting for Chi to take the call, Rydon did something he rarely did, watched television. More than a week later, pictures of the slain students were still all over the news. Seeing their faces sent rage through his body. They were young, innocent, and full of life. Only to have it cut short.

"Rydon, is that you?" Chi called out on the other end of the phone.

"You know it. I have a bone to pick with you, Chi. I thought this was an undercover case? I had folks in Virginia telling *me* when I was *supposed* to arrive in the Carolinas. That's not right, Chi," Rydon spoke calmly.

"I know, brother. Trust me, I had no idea word would spread so quickly. The day I called you, a reporter asked if we would bring in any outsiders to help out with the case. All I told her was that it was an option we thought about pursuing. Her response was and I quote, *Are you talking about Detective Tyme?*" Chi concluded.

"Did you confirm it?" Rydon replied.

"I didn't deny it. I simply said *we're going to explore all avenues to bring peace back to our community*. Once word spread that you were in Virginia, it was pretty much a done deal."

"How did I become a celebrity, Chi? I didn't ask for this," Rydon said.

"It chose you, Rydon, and it fits you well. You should embrace it."

"If it were up to me, I would still be helping folks find their family members," Rydon said, reminiscing on his younger years.

"The good ole days. We'll never get those back," Chi chuckled.

"No time soon. It seems like we walked into a burning building the minute this Civil Rights War began. Well, brother, I'm here now. Where do you need me?"

"Rest easy, I'll brief you in the morning," Chi assured him.

"Perfect, peace."

"Peace, thanks again, Rydon."

As the television set played into the night, Rydon closed his eyes for possibly his last night of full sleep during his stint in the Carolinas.

A knock at the door woke him from his sleep as he quickly sprung to his feet. "Yes?" he answered, peaking through the peephole.

"Good morning, sir. Here is your breakfast. Good day," the service attendant smiled, as the door opened.

"Thank you, good day," Rydon replied.

After breakfast, Rydon clad himself in his new attire, made mostly of either fine silk or Egyptian cotton. Officially taking on his new look for the assignment, Rydon grabbed his Lethal Lenses from the window seal, slid them on his face and out the door he went.

Orangeburg, South Carolina

Orangeburg Police Department

7:15 a.m. Eastern Standard Time

1968 February 17, Saturday

"If it isn't the hardest working man in showbiz," Chi shouted with his arms stretched out in the air, smiling from ear to ear. "Look at you. You look like new money, brother. I can hardly recognize you. Is this the style in HP now? Take me back, ASAP! It's been too long anyway!" Chi laughed, joking with an old friend.

"I'm going back to Michigan. See you later, Chi," Rydon smirked, turning around.

"I'm just joking, brother. Life as a celebrity can't be that bad," Chi laughed, patting Rydon on the back.

"It's the worst, my man. You'd be surprised how crooked some folks are. They smile in your face and talk about you behind your back. To make matters worse, the same folks get on television and act like model citizens. It's sad, brother, it really is," Rydon said, shaking his head.

"I've heard that before but never from the horse's mouth. That's terrible. What hope do we have, if our most visible representation don't care about the people?" Chi asked.

"Call an exhausted Detective named Tyme. I couldn't give up on the people if I tried. My unborn children are rooting for me."

"Right on, brother. That's heavy. They put me in charge to see all this through behind the scenes and whatnot. I told them I'd only do it if I could pick my own team. No ifs, ands, or buts.

"You were my first call, brother. What we're doing here is definitely something your unborns will be proud of," Chi promised.

As the men walked through the precinct catching up on old times, Rydon laughed more with Chi in fifteen minutes than he had all year. Chi was always a breath of fresh air. Rydon enjoyed linking up with his old college roommate, it took him back to simpler times.

Walking into the locker room, Chi grabbed two, oversized duffle bags, giving one to Rydon and holding on to the heavier one with both hands. "I'll be straight forward with you. Things are a lot different down here than it is up north.

"Officer Scott and Sergeant Lynch have already been reprimanded if you want to call it that. During the district investigation, Scott and Lynch were on a paid leave of absence and back to work four days later. Today is their first day away from their desks and back into the field."

"How's the community taking it all?" Rydon asked, unzipping the bag.

"The first few days were chaotic. It was a little better during the investigation but once news broke that they were back on the force, the rioters picked up right where they left off," Chi said.

"It looked pretty peaceful last night," Rydon stated.

"The riots weren't in Orangeburg. Mobs organized and took the riots to Richland County where the two officers live. They tore the neighborhoods up pretty bad too."

"You should have seen the riots in Detroit last year, Chi. It got real ugly. We had to guard the mom and pop stores around the city all night. You know insurance companies will find any reason to reject their claims," Rydon reminisced.

"I knew it was a problem when I saw ball players standing on cars with megaphones. We saw that on the news way out here," Chi recalled.

"*Déjà vu.* So, what's in here?" Rydon asked, unzipping the bag's side pocket.

"I have your armor and firearms in here. Your bag has a pair of shoes, size 11.5, and 11 in boots. Uniforms for the Richland County Police Department, jackets, sweaters, t-shirts, and other paraphernalia. Here's your badge and dog tags," Chi said, handing over the rest of Rydon's hardware.

"Chi, wait a minute. This is an Officer's badge," Rydon said, holding the cold metal. "Chi, this clown is going to be my superior officer? You're joking, right?" Rydon hoped. "The same clown who broke up a bonfire promoting *peace,* with bullets? *He's* my superior officer?" he questioned.

"It's the only way, Rydon. If you have a higher rank, he won't show his true colors. Now, he's going to show you the unfiltered version of Sergeant Lynch... rookie," Chi looked away, hiding his eyes.

"Rookie!?"

Columbia, South Carolina

400th Block of Westshore Road

12:10 p.m. Eastern Standard Time

1968 February 17, Saturday

Vowing to be a part of the people and not apart from it, Rydon was once again in the midst of turmoil. The people in his new neighborhood weren't too fond of his arrival. For the first time in his career, he felt his safety was at risk in the place he called home.

Residing where he worked, Rydon was more than just another new face during turbulent times. In some ways, it made him a target. Unable to be protected or held accountable by his public persona, he had to find peace the best he could.

Keeping his identity concealed like a third-grader on Halloween night, Rydon always seemed to go undetected. No matter how recognizable he may have been, Rydon was the undisputed master of disguise.

Forty-three hours away from another mission, it was almost time to conference with his first lady.

Durham, North Carolina

4130 Liberty Street, Penthouse Suite

5:55 p.m. Eastern Standard Time

1968 February 17, Saturday

Coasting north on I-85, Rydon had more on his hands than an artist after a masterpiece. Lately, he was starting to wonder what life would be like without the associated stressors. He was finally feeling the effects of a possible burnout that his loved ones warned him about for decades.

With a week in the books, it was time to debrief with his favorite field reporter. "You won't believe how dirty they did me, baby," Rydon vented.

"Uh oh, what's up, Ry?" Gabriella asked with her chin rested in the palm of her hand.

"It's my rank. Not only is the perpetrator my superior officer, but Chi has me starting from the bottom. I'm a rookie. A guppy, the new guy, a novice, blank canvas, milky breath. I'm still wet behind the ears, baby.

"I can keep going but I won't. I have to watch my blood pressure just thinking about it. I should have stayed in the U.P. with you," he said, nodding in her direction.

"Then who would be here? You made the right choice, Ry. These people need you. This might be a good thing for you, finally being able to relax while someone else takes the wheel for a change," Gabriella replied.

Many days turned night over the years, Gabriella fell asleep alone, hoping Rydon would be there in the morning. Leaving her faith where it belonged, out of her hands. Instead, she learned to let things work itself out. It was a lot easier on her nerves.

"Everything will fall in place the way it's supposed to, Ry," she assured him.

"I hear you, baby, but you have to remember who his last partner was. Their bad cop, bad cop routine lasted six years. Imagine the filth he fed Officer Scott," he explained, full of disgust.

"That's what I'm saying, Ry. You're going to get the full experience working under him."

"They got you too, Gabby?" Rydon said, shaking his head.

"Got me? What's that supposed to mean?" she wondered.

35

"Everybody keeps saying I'll get the full experience like that makes it any easier."

"What are you saying, Ry?"

"It sounds easy but I have to actually live that life. If my sergeant is crooked what do you think he expects me to be? This is real life, not a movie. I'll have to live with every decision that both of us make," Rydon said, hanging his head at the thought.

"I never thought about it that way, baby. I'm sorry," Gabriella said, lifting his chin.

"Don't be sorry, you're not the problem."

"Well, try not to think about that right now. This might help… guess what I brought?"

"What?"

"It's a secret. I'll show you after you get out of the shower. You smell like a cop, take care of that," she shooed.

After a night filled with ecstasy, the couple slept late into the morning. "Good morning," Gabriella said, smiling as she kissed Rydon's cheek.

"Good morning, you brush your teeth yet," he joked, hugging her tightly.

"I know you're not talking. Your breath smells like yesterday," Gabriella laughed, plugging her nostrils.

Preparing for a day of business and pleasure with his wife and sidekick, Rydon was dressed and ready to go. "You ready yet, babe?" he called out.

"Give me five minutes," Gabriella called from the doorway with five fingers spread as she finished her mascara.

Plopping to the couch, Rydon knew it would be closer to a half-hour before his lady would be ready to depart. He turned on the television set to hear what the people had to say about the area's current events while his wife gussied up.

"In current news, revolutionary detective, Dr. Rydon Tyme was thought to be on his way to the Orangeburg, South Carolina but it seems to have been hearsay. This footage was just released on the Real Newz Network and it appears he's flying high with the Outlaws."

Smiling in admiration at the timing of the release, he walked to the bathroom to gloat about the Superior Seventeen.

"They just released the footage from Douglass University. They still think I'm in the Old Dominion."

"You go, boy," she shouted.

"You're wearing that dress. You make it look like one of a kind," he flirted, squeezing her elbow.

As the highlights concluded, Rydon returned to his seat in front of the television.

"Evelyn is live in Orangeburg, speaking with citizens about the arrival of Detective Tyme. Here's what they had to say about the beloved Dr. Rydon Tyme."

"Thank you, Lacey. Hi, I'm Evelyn Princeton live in Orangeburg with Tim Waters. Mr. Waters, Dr. Tyme is a no show. Does that surprise you at all?"

"It does. Don't say you're going to do something if you're not going to do it. A lot of people were counting on him to help out. Virginia LOTT has helped but it would've been nice to see him," Tim said with disappointment.

"Many citizens in the area are disappointed in Dr. Tyme. We have Susan Cummings, a sophomore here at South Carolina International with us now. Miss Cummings, did you know while you and your community were fighting for equality here in Orangeburg, Dr. Tyme was slam-dunking with students at Douglass University in Virginia?" Evelyn informed the student.

"It doesn't surprise me. I thought he was different. When he came here to speak, he inspired us to stand up for what we believed in. His visit is the reason we're in all this mess in the first place.

"I wish he never came. We lost three innocent people and he's somewhere playing basketball. We don't need Dr. Tyme," Susan said, bawling a stream of tears into the foam windscreen of the microphone.

"And there you have it. Students are irate here in Orangeburg, for more reasons than one. I'm Evelyn Princeton, back to you Lacey."

"Thank you, Evelyn. My how quickly things change, a hero turned zero in less than a month. In other news, the Desires begin their eleven city tour this week. Check your local newspaper for tour dates in a city near you."

Shaking his head vigorously, Rydon became more and more numb to the needs of society. He was losing his motivation and fast. "I'm ready… Ry, what's wrong?" Gabriella asked, suddenly dropping her smile.

"Nothing, I'll be alright."

Mixing business with pleasure, especially over dinner was rumored to be a terrible idea but for Rydon, it provided his only source of happiness. After discussing the upcoming week, the man and wife picked up where they left off over a week ago. Their private party in the Upper Peninsula had officially relocated to Durham, North Carolina.

Blythewood, South Carolina

Richland County Police Department

6:40 a.m. Eastern Standard Time

1968 February 19, Monday

Arriving early on his first day, Rydon was primed and ready to go. As a professional detective, he had to be ready to perform at any time regardless of his emotional state. Arranging things in his locker, Rydon began creating an image in his head for his latest façade as Officer Toussaint.

Fast cars, tractors, fancy clothes, shoes, gold, and silver jewelry became his newest interests. Eager to meet his latest mentor, Detective Rydon Tyme transformed into Officer Len Toussaint as he laced up his boots, anxious for his training day.

Taking a lesson from his protégés, Rydon would only portray an outspoken, flashy, know it all, super rookie. As a professional, he learned how to use his passion and fury to his advantage. However, he felt internally dictated the personality of his undercover image.

When his patience began to wear thin, his undercover portrayals were usually overly outspoken. If his mind was at peace, he took on cases that required an abundance of discipline. It was an effective form of release therapy, allowing him to say exactly what was on his mind.

Making his way toward the coffee pot, Rydon grabbed a packet of ginger-lemon tea, honey, and brown sugar cubes. Mixing the contents in a large black mug, he sipped the steaming herbs as he removed staged pictures, awards, and supplies from a box. He used the last ten minutes of his time, making his desk a little more personal.

"You must be the rookie? I'm Sergeant Lynch. Keep your mouth shut, eyes open, and you may learn a thing or two. If I give you an order, follow it quickly. Hesitation is a sign of fear in the battlegrounds and fear can get you killed. You better not fear anyone besides me out there today. That clear? Any questions?"

"What a joke," Rydon said, bursting out in laughter.

"Come again?" Sergeant Lynch asked, refusing to believe his own ears.

"I'll spell it for you. What… a… J-o-k-e. I don't know what kind of officers you've trained in the past but I'm not them. First off, don't call me 'rookie.' My name is Officer Len Toussaint – always has been."

"Secondly, I fear no man, *especially* not you. Last but not least, I'm from the streets. In the last two years, I went from a hopeless homeless man to graduating at the top of my class at the Justice Academy without help from anyone. I know the streets like the back of my hand. So you tell me who's really a rookie."

"I hope you're as confident a cop, as you are a person. You remind me a lot of myself years ago, Officer Toussaint. As long as you don't act like a rookie, I won't call you one. We have a busy day ahead of us with all the riots in Richland County and protests in Orangeburg.

"You're going to have to take the lead on a lot of things today, so it's good that you're outspoken. Grab your gear and I'll meet you out front—Officer Toussaint, it's time to hit the streets."

Surprised at how well things were going as Officer Toussaint, Rydon could only chuckle to himself. Knowing he only had one shot to convince his superior officer that he wasn't the typical rookie, he succeeded with flying colors.

"Where you from rook—pardon me—Officer Toussaint?" Sergeant Lynch smiled, tipping his hat.

"Harlem."

"A Renaissance Man, no wonder you act the way you do."

"What's that supposed to mean?" Rydon looked with a side eye.

"A cocky, rookie hotshot. Probably trigger happy too," Officer Lynch smirked, eerily.

"You think you have me figured out, huh, Sergeant?" Rydon dismissed.

"Read you like a book. Good news, I'm the same way. Stick with me, Officer Toussaint, and you'll make Sergeant in no time."

"What's no time?"

"I'll be up for Lieutenant in a few years, leaving my spot open for you if you want it," Sergeant Lynch nodded. "If and only if, you walk as good as you talk."

"You think so?"

"In this town, it's not what you know but who *and* what you know. You have what it takes, I can already see that. Now, you just have to prove it."

As the words *prove it* rolled off Sergeant Lynch's tongue, Rydon began feeling queasy. He could only imagine who else heard those words under Sergeant Lynch's watch. Gazing out the window of the squad car, Rydon was prepared to expect the unexpected.

"All available units are requested in Columbia for a 594. I repeat all available units, we have a 594 in progress in Columbia, copy if you can," the CB radio blared.

"Officer Toussaint, go ahead and take your first call for action," Sergeant Lynch said with a smirk.

Rydon picked up the receiver, "Sergeant Lynch and Officer Toussaint are on it. Copy that."

"Roger that," the operator responded.

Columbia, South Carolina

8:05 a.m. Eastern Standard Time

1968 February 19, Monday

Turning down Park Street, searching for a parking spot, people were scattered in every direction, going haywire. The riots had become very organized over the last couple of weeks. No one knew where the mobs would strike next or what time during the day.

When Sergeant Lynch and Officer Toussaint arrived at the scene, it was near impossible to determine who to protect and who to serve. The area was always congested with people. It was most notable for its shopping districts in the neighborhood. Patrons bought clothes, electronics, and groceries all in the same quarters.

"I have to be upfront with you, Officer Toussaint. It's a lot different down here than it is up north," Sergeant Lynch said sternly.

"I keep hearing that, but what does it mean?"

"Some of these people are savages. The only time they help each other is to riot. Force is the only thing they understand. Every now and then, we have to make an example out of one of them," Sergeant Lynch said, keeping an eye on the car in the rearview mirror.

"Back in Harlem, folks only rioted when they were victimized by the boys in blue. Or civil rights violations, believe it or not. A few years back in '64, it got really ugly after a Lieutenant shot and killed a high school kid--- Why are these folks so angry? People forget to ask themselves that during every riot..." Rydon said, leaving food for thought as Sergeant Lynch eased into an open parking spot.

After asking the million-dollar question, their conversation was interrupted by liquid splashing against the windows. Loud bangs thumped off the doors, trapping the officers inside while the mob doused the vehicle in red, white, and blue paint.

"See what I mean, Officer Toussaint!?"

"Pull off! It's coving the windshield!" Rydon yelled to a sergeant in shock.

"I can barely see!" Sergeant Lynch said, nervously triggering the windshield wipers, smearing mixed paint across the glass of the squad car. Sergeant Lynch's blind peel out only made things worse as he sped off toward an open field.

"Watch out for that tree!" Rydon roared.

———

Exiting the wrecked car, there was no one in sight. The rioters involved managed to escape the premises leaving authorities in disarray. The department issued Pentagon Bullet was covered in paint, halted in its tracks by a large oak tree. Sergeant Lynch and Officer Toussaint were puzzled by the latest happenings in Columbia, South Carolina.

"Officer Toussaint, call in a 504 to dispatch. I'm going to check the premises. Yell if you need me."

"Affirmative… We have a 504 in progress on Park Street, south of Washington. Rioters may have totaled our squad car," Rydon alerted the operator.

"Identify yourself," the voice prompted.

"Officer Len Toussaint, badge number 7454852, Richland County."

"Who's your superior officer?"

"Sergeant Christopher Lynch."

"Copy, Officer Toussaint. A 1968 Pentagon Sun will be delivered to 3014 Assembly Street. The title of the vehicle will remain in Sergeant Lynch's name. Detectives will bring the paperwork with them when they arrive for questioning."

"Roger that," Rydon replied.

From afar, Rydon could see Sergeant Lynch was one to judge a book by its cover. A group of seven men laid stretched out on the arid, February cement. Cited for suspicious activity. With his boot on the back of one of the youngsters, Sergeant Lynch looked up to see his new apprentice walking toward them.

"Look what I found Officer," Sergeant Lynch pointed to the ground with his foot on a man's back.

"What do we have here, Sergeant?" Rydon wondered, hoping the situation could be explained.

"Trash on the concrete, seven pieces of trash and I know this one here had something to do with our new paint job," Sergeant Lynch said, driving his boot in the man's back.

"I just came from the store. I didn't have anything to do with it," the man grunted.

"Shut up! I know it was you. It was probably all of you," growled Sergeant Lynch.

"You, with the boot on his back, I don't care if you move so fast it makes Sergeant Lynch fall. But you need to get over here, immediately," Rydon demanded, calmly masking his emotions. "I'm only going to say that once," he said in a deep, intimidating tone.

"Yes, Officer," the man said in relief, standing up from the ground. If disrespect had a face, it stood in front of Rydon, wondering what he was going to do next.

"What did you see? I only ask questions once and that's the last time I'm going to warn you. If you send me on a wild goose chase, you'll be scared of geese for the rest of your life. You understand me?" Rydon warned.

"Yes, sir."

"I'm listening," Rydon reminded him.

"I was on my way to work, waiting on bus number eight. I saw you two pull up and park. After they threw paint on your car and you hit the tree, everyone ran away."

"Don't lie to me. You just said you were in the store!" Rydon grunted.

"No sir, I did go to the store after you crashed. I have the receipt in my pocket if you don't believe me."

"I don't believe you. Why didn't you help us instead of leaving for snacks?" Rydon wondered, seeing no holes in the man's story.

"Why would I help you? You don't help us. You just rough us up and act like folks don't have a reason to riot. He just had his foot on my back calling me a piece of trash. Can I leave now? I still have a bus to catch."

"What happened to the other squad cars?"

"What squad cars? Police don't come to Parkwood," the man replied.

"You, get to work. The rest of you get up and stand on the wall," Rydon instructed, taking over the situation.

Chapel Hill, North Carolina

11:10 a.m. Eastern Standard Time

1968 February 24, Saturday

Merging onto I-77, Rydon felt a weight lifted from his shoulders. Three hours into his drive, he finally felt like himself again. Portraying someone with his opposite personality was becoming a little too easy.

The hard part appeared to be switching back to his normal self. After a full work week as Officer Len Toussaint, Rydon found himself becoming the character he played more and more with each passing day.

Reaching exit 266, it was time to converse in his native tongue. "Welcome to Black House Suites at Chapel Hill, sir. How may we assist you?"

"Thank you, I feel welcomed. It looks really nice in here." Rydon said, admiring the chandeliers in the lobby.

"Glad to hear, I'll let the manager know we must be doing something right these days," the man grinned.

"Could you call Gabriella Tyme and let her know Officer Len Toussaint is here. She's staying in the penthouse suite."

The hotel assistant picked up the phone to complete the request "Hello Mrs. Tyme, you have a visit from an Officer Len Toussaint. He's asking that you come downstairs. Okay, bye-bye. She'll be right down," he replied with a smile.

"Thank you," Rydon said, patting his hands on the counter.

"You're welcome. Enjoy your day."

As the elevator opened, Gabriella entered the lobby in a complete frenzy. "Ry, don't do that! I was expecting bad news," Gabriella said, hitting her husband's arm. "I just knew you were a policeman from South Carolina coming all this way to ruin my jazzy day."

"You know I'll always be alright even when I'm not," he said, smiling, looking into her eyes. Kissing her temple, Gabriella buried her body in Rydon's arms.

Tracing the bridge of Rydon's nose, down to the top of his chest, Gabriella felt what she thought was lost. "I love your beard. It's filling in fast," she said, pausing. "I don't think you've shaved since we left to go ice skating in the U.P., come to think of it," Gabriella pondered.

45

"I haven't," Rydon chuckled.

"Is that gold around your neck, twice? When did you get so flashy? It's on your fingers and wrists too," grabbing his forearms, Gabriella couldn't help but admire Rydon's new look.

"That's a nice bracelet. Who are you?" she said, grinning.

"I'm Officer Len Toussaint, nice to meet you, ma'am," he said, tipping his invisible hat."

"Don't make me blush... I forgot how big your head was," she giggled, rubbing Rydon's smooth, shaved bald head.

Rydon's jaw dropped as he gasped for air. "Nooooo Ry, in a good way. It fits your body. Really, Baby. This is a good look on you," Gabriella said, taking pictures without a camera. "I've been telling you for years to spoil yourself a little. It's about time you took my advice," she said, holding his chin in her hands.

"I feel like Cato mixed with a little Master Haji and Lahal the Great."

"Cato I understand, he's your alter ego for sure but Master Haji and Lahal the Great? That a stretch, baby. I've been working in the Carolinas and we have never heard of an Officer Len Toussaint," Gabriella whispered, tapping his chest. "People know about the Terrific Two in Antarctica."

"You're right, I take that back," Rydon said respecting her truth.

"But... they know who Dr. Rydon Tyme is in Antarctica too," she blushed, playing with her curly brown hair.

"You always know what to say," Rydon said, kissing her cheek, taking her hand as they left for the parking lot.

"Now, I'm saying *business first.* You picked a great time to send me here," Gabriella said with new, news on the way.

"Really what did you do?"

"Riot," she replied.

"Wait, what?" he responded, quickly.

"The family you arranged for me, were getting ready to riot when I got there."

"Speak English, Gabby," Rydon said, opening the door for his lady.

"How can I put this? I was a part of a riot," Gabriella said as she shrugged, buckling her seatbelt.

"A riot or a protest? Please explain. I'm all ears," Rydon said, extending his ear with his first two fingers behind it.

"When I got to Chapel Hill, the Garnet residence wasn't home. Luckily, they told their neighbors I was coming and left a key for me. They came home so loud they woke me while I was sleeping on the couch," Gabriella pouted.

"That's the Garnet's for sure," Rydon chuckled.

"They came in with the cutest little twins I ever did see," Gabriella reminisced. "The Garnet's told me how long you all have known each other and some of the crazy things you all did in college," she said, raising her eyebrow.

"They told you all that?" Rydon wondered, uncertain of the things she may have learned from the glory days he often mentioned.

"You were only sixteen, Ry. How did you keep up with them?"

"How did they keep up with me is the better question. I was a completely different student in undergrad than I was when we met in grad school."

"I heard you were a party animal! I would have never guessed!" Gabriella laughed, clapping her hands, kicking her feet from her seat.

"People always told me college was where you had *the most fun of your life*. That's why I finished secondary school so fast, it was slow motion."

"Enough about me, you're with me for life. We can talk about this anytime. What happened with the riot, baby? I'm on the edge of my seat over here, *and* I'm still not sure how to react."

"K. Well, the next day, they told me where they were the night I got there. Things are a lot different down here than up north."

"Everyone keeps saying that. Keep going, I'm sorry," Rydon said, waving his hands.

"As I was saying. It's a lot different. Up north, folks just look at you funny, like they're jealous of us. Down here, it's the opposite. They act like they're better than us. As if we don't breathe the same air and drink the same water. And they *will* tell you how they feel.

"Speaking of water, folks drink from different water fountains and I'll let you guess whose looked best, she said with a smirk. "I switched the signs at every fountain I drank at. I know that much."

"Me too," Rydon laughed. We're probably wanted in at least two counties."

"You're so silly," she giggled. "I wouldn't doubt it. We couldn't go to any restaurants downtown; we had to go to places in the neighborhood. The food was delicious, really good. They took me to a place called Messy Vesey's, best barbeque I've had in a long time.

"During the day, they showed me around the city and all the places we couldn't go. I heard people say with my own ears, that they didn't serve our kind, can you believe it? It's 1968, you'd think things would have changed by now," Gabriella said, with her eyebrows nearly touching as she searched through her purse.

"At night, we roamed the streets, talking to folks who were rioting and just asked them why they were out there," Gabriella said, filing her nails.

"That is *not* what I meant when I told you to ask people about the riots, baby. I was talking about at the mall or the grocery store. Even the library, but not in the middle of a riot!"

"You don't have to raise your voice at me, Rydon Mahdi Tyme," Gabriella frowned.

"All I'm saying is that inexperienced rioters are usually the ones who wind up getting hurt. It's an art to everything Gabriella Zaina Tyme," he lectured, kissing her cheek. "You can't just walk around in a warzone even if you are with the Garnet's."

"Well, find me a hotel next time then," Gabriella rolled her eyes.

"Fine, I will."

"Well fine, then!"

"Fine."

"Fine, fine, fine!"

"You're so goofy, I can't stay mad at you. Come here," Rydon chuckled, pulling her in for a kiss.

"I really do want you to stay away from these riots. Daytime protests are fine as long as you aren't by yourself. The riots are spreading fast and at night, everyone looks the same to some folk."

"Okay, man, I'll stay away from riots. How was your week, Officer Toussaint?" Gabriella blushed, rubbing his shaven head.

"It was fast. Lynch told me I'll have to start taking the lead from here on out, not knowing this is what I do," Rydon answered.

"You go, boy!" she rooted.

"My first day on the job, we got a call for malicious mischief in Columbia. That's about twenty minutes or so from Richland County where I'm living nowadays."

"Is that cop lingo for a riot?" Gabriella wondered, hoping she was able to keep up.

"Bingo! We pulled up to the scene, parked. A minute later, tops," Rydon said, snapping his fingers. "They threw paint on the windows and beat on our doors. We pulled off right into a tree. After that, Lynch had some fellas laying on the ground calling them trash, blaming them for everything."

"See what I mean? It's different down here. Did you do something about it?"

"Does silver shine? Of course, I did. I can't blow my cover day one but I neutralized the situation. He had his boot on the back of one of them, so I called him over first.

"I felt like he was trying to tell me something and he was. He had to get to work. I sent him on his way and told the rest of them to stand up. It's no telling what would have happened if I wasn't there. Lynch thought I did great. He said I showed initiative all week. The man has no clue who he's dealing with.

"We patrolled the area on foot and met up with some detectives who asked us about it all then gave us a new squad car. It felt strange being a student to those types of people. They prioritize different things.

"I love money as much as the next guy but it's more to life than money and power. All they talked about was how to undercut the next man for his spot. You're right it is different. It's a dog eat dog world in the south."

Columbia, South Carolina

400th Block of Westshore Road

5:04 a.m. Eastern Standard Time

1968 February 28, Wednesday

Rydon picked up the phone that interrupted his sleep with a raspy, "Hello?

"We need to talk."

"Chi?"

"Meet me at the diner in a half hour. I'm on the road now."

Climbing out of bed, Rydon showered and dressed for the day. Strapping his bulletproof vest, buttoning his shirt, and shielding his eyes with customized frames, he left the house with twenty minutes to spare.

Rydon sat in the corner of Westshore's eldest restaurants, *Eggs, and Waffles*; named for the first item on the diner's menu. It was there he stirred a cup of hot tea, forking down a steak and eggs combination.

Rydon waited patiently, reading the newspaper in the middle of his meal. A veteran on the job, dressed in a uniform designed for a rookie. Major Chi, however, entered the breakfast spot decorated with accolades, stealing the attention of everyone in the place. "Rydon," he greeted with a firm handshake. "Do not take this to the station," Chi said, handing him a package.

"Keep it down Chi, someone might hear you. The name is Officer Len Toussaint. You know that."

"Toussaint!" Chi shouted with a loud clap. "How could I forget to use a name like that."

"How long have you been a morning person, I didn't know you could wake up this early. I'd be done with classes for the day before you woke up back in college," Rydon chuckled.

"Man," Chi said, shaking his head.

"What's this about?" Rydon asked, thumbing through the files.

"I can't say… That way we can never put each other in the middle of all of this if folks start connecting dots. Use it however you can. Rookies can't get this kind of intel," Chi laughed while Rydon waited for the joke to be over.

"You done?" Rydon replied, mocking Chi's laugh.

"Seriously though, Everything you need to know is in that envelope. Whatever you do, don't take it to the station," Chi reminded him.

"Don't take it to the station, check," Rydon agreed, stuffing the envelope inside a zipped leather folder.

Augusta, Georgia

Interstate 20 West

11:11 a.m. Eastern Standard Time

1968 March 2, Saturday

Augusta was in the same situation as many other states in the south. Citizens were bruised physically and drained emotionally. Passing a billboard of the state's motto, "Wisdom, justice, moderation," Rydon could only hope the quote would hold true during the upcoming week.

He reached Macon, Georgia around 2:00 p.m. and headed to the residence of a family friend who opened their doors to his wife during her travels. Their high-profile image put her in harms way without his accommodations. His family and friends were the only people he trusted in that part of the south.

Although Rydon switched states, little changed. The tension in the air was so thick, it was almost visible. Signaling his turn, Rydon parked his truck into an overcrowded driveway. He pounded on the foundation of the house, hoping to overpower the laughter taking place on the other side of the door. "Rydon Tyme! Get in here, brother!" Travis motioned from the doorway.

"Travis Watts! What's shaking?" Rydon replied with a man hug.

"I haven't seen you in over a decade. How's life?"

"Life has been a roller coaster. Some days are up, some down. I get paid to add problems to my universe. After a while, no matter how much I make, I never get to enjoy it because I'm always worrying about the people. It's my curse."

"I can't tell. Your jewels are glistening."

"Money doesn't make the man, the man makes the money," Rydon shrugged.

"You've been saying that since college. Did the stress go to your hair, what happened up top?" Travis said, pointing to Rydon's head.

"Be easy man, my hair grows faster than Amazon grass. I cut it for work-related reasons," he joked.

"Come on in, brother, let me show you the house. Speaking of college, we were just telling Gabby about the time you told Maxine and Christine your name was Corduroy Lucas. When I say the name stuck, you would have thought he said his name was Velcro," Travis said, falling to the couch in laughter, holding his stomach.

"Aw man, I forgot about that. Gabby, don't you get any ideas," Rydon laughed, pointing to his wife.

"I won't Corduroy, I mean, Ry, I mean Len. Wait, I'm *so* confused?" she said before tears left her eyes.

As the room filled with laughter and memories, it may have been the only harmonic atmosphere in the entire neighborhood.

"Let me tell you about this man here. One time we were at a house party in San Diego after an away track meet and the guys we just dusted on the track couldn't stop running off at the mouth. Rydon said and I'll never forget it, *Are y'all trying to lose twice today, or you just gon keep talking?* Next thing you know we were outside racing in the street like teenagers. Rydon Tyme, the man backed up every word he spoke!"

Macon, Georgia

Interstate 20 West

10:07 p.m. Eastern Standard Time

1968 March 2, Saturday

After sunset and the festivities ended, tension seemed to naturally resurface in the air. Conversations were no longer about the times that were but the times that should be.

"It seems timid here, Trav. How do you like living in Macon? Especially having sons," Rydon asked, needing a feel for his surroundings.

"Timid? The word is *oppressed*. They call the mayor Machine Gun for goodness sake," Travis said. "I just have to be strong for my boys. Then they'll see it as the only way to be."

"Real spill," Rydon agreed. "What's up with the mayor, Machine Gun? Is he a veteran?" Rydon wondered.

"I don't want to talk about it but he's the Colonel of Macon during this Civil Rights War, that's for sure," Travis said, angered by it all

"I've heard a lot of horror stories about these power struck, money-hungry oppressors. How did this guy get a name like that?" Rydon asked with intrigue.

"I don't know if you want to know."

"I asked, didn't I?" Rydon bounced back, raising his eyebrow.

"Riots have been breaking out across the south, state by state. The mayor instructed policemen to shoot to kill if necessary when dealing with looters. He put billboards up around the city warning citizens that they would be shot on sight if caught in armed robberies. I bet the man has never been in a fistfight and he's giving orders to have folks killed."

"What a coward."

"You'd be surprised how ignorant some folks are here, brother."

Blythewood, South Carolina

Richland County Police Department

7:15am Eastern Standard Time

1968 March 4, Monday

With Gabriella safely residing with the Watts residence, Rydon's mind was at peace. Every family on the list of cities earned his trust in many ways through the years.

Back on the clock in Richland County, leaving for work early and staying late was becoming a habit again. Taking lead with Sergeant Lynch meant paperwork, paperwork, and more paperwork for Officer Toussaint. Sergeant Lynch was the point man on many missions, knowing he could pass on administrative responsibilities to his latest officer in training.

Every morning for twenty minutes, Rydon mentally prepared for the day ahead of him. No other two-week span of his life was riddled with so much chaos. Word spread long ago about the injustices of the south but the daily reminders brought it all home for him.

"Officer Toussaint, did you finish the write up on the traffic stop from yesterday?" Sergeant Lynch asked, sipping his coffee.

"I was getting ready to drop it off on your desk, Sergeant," Rydon said, holding a manila folder, as he entered Sergeant Lynch's cubicle.

"It's finished already? Officer Toussaint, you are a machine. You work like a seasoned veteran."

"Thank you, Sergeant but to answer your question, I'm not finished. I didn't know what to write. A day later, I still don't know what the kid did," Rydon said confused by the situation.

"Officer Toussaint, you are out of line. I gave you three offenses to choose from. Reckless driving, speeding, or illegal parking, make a choice, rookie," Sergeant Lynch frowned.

"Look here… Christopher, I'm not a liar. You pulled him over for no reason, threw him against the squad car for no reason, and you had him in handcuffs thirty minutes too long, for no reason! If you want to cover up your bad police work, write your own paperwork," Rydon said, intensely dropping the folder on Sergeant Lynch's desk.

"What's going on in here?" Captain Drew commanded as he entered the conversation without request.

"I don't know Captain, ask Sergeant," Rydon responded first.

55

"Sergeant, what's the problem?"

"Officer Toussaint has a problem accepting orders from his superior officers," Sergeant Lynch pointed.

"Officer Toussaint?"

"I'm not the one with the problem and you better watch that finger," Rydon snapped back, losing control of his temper.

"Good, issue resolved. Sergeant, watch the finger... Officer Toussaint, you've been doing a great job here so far," Captain Drew said, shaking Rydon's hand. "I know it can be hard following orders sometimes but Sergeant Lynch has been at this for a long time. I don't know the specifics of this incident, but you must follow direct orders coming from whoever is in charge, am I understood?"

"I hear you loud and clear, Captain."

Having lost his latest battle, Rydon had every intention of winning the war. With a chip on his shoulder for the day, he insisted on giving Sergeant Lynch a dose of his own medicine for the rest of his stay in Richland County, South Carolina.

With talking being at a minimum, Sergeant felt it was time to break the ice during the last patrol of the day. "Officer Toussaint, I know you might not understand how things are in the south, but we are in a state of emergency. We must be proactive. I'll repeat that. We must be proactive.

"Yesterday, for instance, you say he did nothing wrong. While that may be true, he may have. Our traffic stop may have saved someone's life. That one-stop made him reconsider every action he made for the rest of the day, I can promise you that," Sergeant Lynch Smirked, tipping his hat.

"What about this guy next to us at the longest red light I've ever sat through?"

"He wouldn't hurt a fly," Sergeant Lynch chuckled.

"What about this man crossing the street?"

"Nine times out of ten, he's already guilty of something, or he will be soon."

"Based on what?"

"Based on experience, Officer Toussaint."

Columbia, South Carolina

400th Block of Westshore Road

9:06 p.m. Eastern Standard Time

1968 March 7, Thursday

Growing more frustrated with the leadership of his commanding officer, Rydon began jogging after his shifts to relieve stress. Rounding Oakwood Drive, he saw a crowd of boys who seemed to be up to no good, huddled around a large duffle bag.

"Kind of chilly tonight, huh fellas?" Rydon asked, catching his breath. "What are you all doing outside so late?" he wondered as the sound of heavy metals crashed to the ground.

"Minding our business, what are you doing outside so late?" one of the boys asked.

"Winding down from work, thanks for asking. I'm a police officer. I have a lot of steam to blow off these days," Rydon said, removing his badge from beneath his hoody.

"Here we go again," the young man dragged, locking his hands behind his head as he dropped to a knee.

"What are you doing? Why are you all lying down on the ground? Get up!" Rydon barked, having a severe case of déjà vu.

"You were going to tell us to do it anyway then check us for weapons. Some of you plant stuff on us just to lock us up. You can't be too much different than the rest of them," another young man chimed in.

"I'm not from around here. I'm completely different from the rest of them," Rydon assured them.

"It sounds nice," the young man responded sarcastically.

"You know what, brother? Over the last few weeks, if I haven't learned anything here, I've learned that's half the reason they give you all such a hard time."

"What's that?"

"Your attitude, that's what. Don't take that the wrong way either because I have the same attitude. When you feel disrespected, you speak up about it, me too *and* I carry a gun. That's why I wear my badge. It diffuses a lot of situations.

"You boys don't have badges and when you apply pressure, it shocks them because they expect you to comply. Attitude and poor judgment," Rydon said, motioning left to right with his hands. Attitude and poor judgment are the prerequisites for trouble around here. If you ever notice, when you talk back, the first place their hand goes is where?" Rydon asked.

"Their hip," the oldest of the group said, leaning on an old wall that bordered Freeman Field.

"Yup, they pop the buckle on that holster," another responded, jumping to a seat atop the wall.

"It's poor judgement under pressure, brother," Rydon spoke.

"That makes sense."

"It makes NO sense," Rydon rejected. "Don't justify the way they treat you. I'm just giving you all the *why*," he said with air quotes. "Now, I do have a question for you all. How many times has an officer told you to get down with your hands behind your head like that?"

"You mean this week or total?" one young man joked, laughing at his pain.

"What do you mean this week, it happens that much?" Rydon asked, still confused.

"Officer, they treat us like dogs around here," he explained in simpler terms.

"Worse than dogs!" another added. "Try doing what they do to us to a dog and I bet you end up doing time."

"Hard time," said the group's leader.

"One cop calls us trash like it's our name. He's the worst of them all. The other cops seem to feed off him."

"Really?" Rydon asked, reaching for his wallet. "Here, I'm Officer Len," he said passing out business cards. "Let me know if anybody abuses the badge around here. What's your name fellas?" Rydon asked, having officially introduced himself.

"I'm David," one young man said, sitting the duffle bag to the side as he reached for Rydon's card. "And that's my brother, Deion," he motioned to the right.

Pushing himself off the wall, Deion nodded his head and took a card.

Over the next hour, Rydon went from frustrated to furious. The horrors of reality made him shudder after conversing with the boys. He knew his next course of action had to be carefully planned; it was almost time to make a case.

Jacob City, Florida

Jacob Main Street

1:11 p.m. Eastern Standard Time

1968 March 9, Saturday

Picket signs, police escorts, and large groups of peaceful protestors scattered the streets, delaying Rydon's estimated time of arrival. Riding through Jacob City, Florida, he felt a refreshing sensation take over his body.

Finally reaching a farm in the boondocks of Jacob City, he parked behind his wife's car as she greeted him from the porch.

"Ry, you're late," she shouted through her hands turned megaphone.

"I know, I was in the middle of a labor strike a few miles back," Rydon said, entering a house decorated with antique furniture and hand-crafted pottery.

An older gentleman entered the living room from the kitchen and greeted him sternly. "If your wife didn't come visit, then you wouldn't have come either, is that what I'm witnessing?"

"Uncle Jeremiah, now you know that's not true," Rydon said with a boyish grin.

"You're so busy trying to save the world, you forgot about your favorite uncle."

"Tell me about it! After this case, I'm going to take a break for a while and I'll make sure you and Aunt Denise are right there with us wherever we go."

"You, take a break? The same young man who used to teach himself during summer vacations growing up. You want us to believe that you, of all people, is going to take a break? I'll believe it when I'm waving goodbye to America from the Atlantic Ocean on this boat I keep hearing about," Uncle Jeremiah said smiling, waving his hand in the middle of his own fantasy.

"It's really nice, Uncle J," Gabriella chimed in.

"*It* has a name," Rydon informed the room. "And the S.S. Success isn't that bad I guess," he said, chuckling with a shrug.

"Cuba, Haiti, Dominican Republic, the Bahamas, Jamaica, where we going?" Rydon said, daydreaming with his uncle.

"I love all those places but I've never been to South America," he said, taking a seat.

"It's a deal. After I wrap this case, I'm going to have my mother send you the dates."

"Don't threaten me with a good time, Rydon," Uncle Jeremiah said, extending the recliner.

"Have I ever let you down, Uncle Jeremiah?"

"No and don't start now," he said, pointing with a rolled-up newspaper.

Being cursed by perfection, Rydon accomplished every goal he ever set, every time. That success rate followed him through school and into his career as a private detective. People around him always expected great things and he never let them down. But there were very few people he could count on for the same luxury. "What's the strike about?" he wondered, changing the subject. "I saw protestors all around the city on my way."

"Teachers resigned statewide," the retired principal clapped. "The news says it's over thirty thousand of them. They're tired of being mistreated. This is their time to be heard," Uncle Jerimiah smiled proudly from his Thinking Man recliner.

Activism was nothing new to Rydon. Generation after generation, Tyme Men were expected to find problems with the world and choose a career in their identified field of need. Uncle Jeremiah's first choice was education.

"Mistreated? How so? I thought everyone loved Teachers. They care, all the time. What are they asking for?"

"Smaller class sizes, safer buildings, after school programs, and higher pay. Those are the main things. Most of them have to buy their own supplies," Uncle Jeremiah said, putting on his reading glasses to look at the newspaper.

"So what's the problem? As much as they sacrifice, give them what they want," Rydon replied.

"Your Aunt and I were saying the same thing but you know how the media is. They slander the people who really care and glamorize the crooks," he vented, clinching the business section tightly with both hands. "Are your boys still in Orangeburg? We need a Real Newz crew here to showcase some of Jacob City's finest."

"That's a good idea, I'll get on it. I can have the camera crew fly down. We can issue a statement as supporters for Educators tomorrow before I head back to the Carolinas. It'll look good for my case undercover too. You're a genius, Uncle Jeremiah."

"Thank you, it's in our bloodline, nephew. I'll let you two catch up before Gabriella gets the same feeling of abandonment that you give us." Uncle Jeremiah faded upstairs while Mr. and Mrs. Tyme slipped out the door and into the farmlands.

"So this is the farm you always talk about?" Gabriella said with wandering eyes.

"Yes ma'am! My cousins and I used to have a ball right where we are now. Uncle Jeremiah never let us have fun until we finished our work for the day. We used to pull weeds right over there," Rydon pointed out.

"That's where we used to milk the cows and gather chicken eggs," he said, motioning toward the barn. "After that, he would let us play here and over there by the stable with the horses."

"Can you ride one?" Gabriella asked.

"Are whales wet? Of course, we used to race all the time."

"I mean right now, not back in the thirties old man," Gabriella giggled, rolling her eyes.

"Old? I'm only forty-two. I'm just entering my prime, Mrs. Tyme. When you get to be my age I will be reminding you of the O-word you just sent my way."

"I'll be old in seven years too, old man."

Wrapping his wife in his arms, he playfully fell with her to the turf. Repositioning herself between his legs, they gazed at the sun bursting its way through the clouds.

"Be careful baby, I'm fragile," Gabriella said with soft eyes.

"Fragile? You're the strongest person I know," he refuted.

"Maybe before, but for the next eight months, I'm as delicate as a rose petal," she blushed.

"Eight months?" Rydon wondered.

"One down, eight to go," she answered with four fingers extended on both hands.

"Eight months, why not just say November, wait, eight and one is nine months. You're pregnant?" Rydon smiled, glowing from cheek to cheek.

"We're pregnant," she answered, playing with his beard.

I'm going to be a father!" Rydon shouted with his fists high in the sky, flashing a smile bright enough to match the setting sun in front of him.

Blythewood, South Carolina

Richland County Police Department

10:31 p.m. Eastern Standard Time

1968 March 14, Thursday

"What did you get into over the weekend Officer Toussaint? You've been on cloud nine all week."

"Nothing much, Sergeant. I ran around my neighborhood a few times so that you don't drive me insane," Rydon answered, keeping business separate from personal.

"I have that effect on people," he smirked. Chuckling at himself, Sergeant Lynch left the cubicle for a cup of coffee. Upon his return, his smile was replaced with a look of disgust. "Get dressed Officer Toussaint. We have a 459 alpha in progress."

Sergeant Lynch raced through the streets, veering in traffic like a mad man. As the scenery began to look more and more familiar, Rydon was grounded from his high identifying the neighborhood as his very own.

Jumping out of the Pentagon Sun squad car, Rydon kept his thoughts to himself, approaching the scene with caution. He kept his eye on his partner more than the streets. Just as he tucked his jewelry inside his bulletproof vest, the duo took off crouching down between the vehicles.

"Back up is on the way. Take the back of the building off the alley, and I'll make my move up front," Sergeant Lynch ordered.

"I don't think it's a good idea to split up Sergeant. Not with just two of us on the scene," Rydon reasoned.

"If you're scared, go home," Sergeant Lynch rejected. "They don't pay you to think, that's why I'm here. Go to the back off the alley and I'll take the front. That's an order, rookie, go!" Sergeant lynch commanded.

Creeping to the alley without making a sound, the fire inside him needed to be released. With adrenaline rushing through his body, Rydon's hands began to tremble. Reaching the back door of the storefront, he stood beside it, leaning against the wall. Blending in with the night.

Phoomp! the door opened, causing Rydon to choose whether he would fight or flight in less than a split second. "Freeze, don't move!" he shouted, unbuckling the strap that secured his pistol.

"I didn't do that, it was already open," The figured responded, covered in darkness.

"The alarm was triggered, and this place is closed, right? Are you working?" Rydon questioned calmly. Inching closer, reaching for his flashlight. "If not, that's a crime. When you commit a crime, you have to come with us. If you're innocent, justice will prevail. Until then, you have the right to remain silent. Anything you say or do may be used against you in the court of law."

"Can I run instead?" the man's arrogance gave him just enough time to let his feet finish the conversation.

As the suspect disappeared, Rydon was stunned. His partner's presence at the end of the alleyway brought him back to the real world. Rydon chased the suspect, throwing him to the ground at the sound of a loud bang.

BOOM!

Standing with his legs shoulder-width apart, Sergeant Lynch had a smoking gun drawn and fired, yards away from the scuffle. Placing handcuffs on the suspect, Rydon rolled the man over.

"David?" Rydon said, making out the young man's face. "You all were casing the place the other night and on top of that you wasted an hour of my time!" Rydon shouted with a fistful of David's shirt in his hands. "You're way too young to be caught up like this. You better hope the old man doesn't press charges!" he grunted.

"You know this piece of trash, Officer?"

Walking toward the squad car, Rydon finished reading David his Miranda rights. Rydon's eyes cut into Sergeant Lynch for the last time without action on his end.

Driving back to the station for booking, the car was silent enough to hear a pin drop. Upon arrival at the station, the Richland County Police Department boomed with applause, acknowledging Officer Toussaint's first arrest, the celebration slowly faded when his face failed to relax and live in the moment.

Searching for his commanding officer after booking, Rydon checked the break room first. Sergeant Lynch's voice could be heard from around the bend by the water cooler.

If the walls of the break room could talk, the stories it would tell. "Next thing I know, I saw two bucks running down the alley. You know me, I shoot first and ask questions later," Sergeant Lynch bragged as the room exploded with laughter and applause.

"Sergeant Lynch, I need a word with you," Rydon requested.

"I'll be there in a minute, rookie," Sergeant Lynch said, dismissing Rydon to finish the story.

"That wasn't a question, Christopher," he rejected the delay, rubbing his beard. "Let's go, now!" Rydon roared.

Exiting the room like a child headed to the principal's office, Sergeant Lynch appeared as if he met his match. As his colleagues and superior officers looked on to see how he would handle the situation, Sergeant Lynch never looked back at their reactions.

Slamming the door behind him, all eyes and ears were glued to the empty corner office of the precinct. "What was that about? You almost shot me out there!" Rydon yelled.

"I never miss, Officer Toussaint. I was shooting at him, not you. If you didn't throw him to the ground like that, you would know, I saved your life."

"You saved my life, when was I in danger?" Rydon asked baffled by the entire conversation.

"The minute you chased after the perpetrator. You're not up north, Officer Toussaint. I keep trying to tell you that! He was luring you into a trap. As soon as you chased him into the darkness, the other thugs he came with would have pounced on you but I scared them off. You're welcome," Sergeant Lynch said loud enough to be heard in the hallway.

"You think this is a game!? This isn't a game, Christopher. That's someone's son and brother you almost killed for no reason. Did you see how I apprehended the suspect without using deadly force? That's police work! Something you know nothing about. Shooting someone doesn't make you a cop. We're here to protect and serve, not to shoot first and ask questions later!" Rydon scolded.

"What are you two screaming about now?" Captain Drew called out as he entered the room, having heard enough.

"Officer Toussaint's naivety almost got him in a lot of trouble. He's delirious. I think he forgets what state he's in sometimes, Captain."

"Captain, he almost shot me. I was going after a suspect and as I took him to the ground, a bullet flew over our heads. He's a loose cannon!"

"Sergeant, is this true?"

"Partially, I fired a shot at the suspect, not Officer Toussaint," Sergeant Lynch said in short.

66

"I want a full report from both of you on my desk by sunrise. Whatever disagreements you have, handle it or take it outside. If I have to talk to you two about keeping the peace in this precinct one more time, both of you will be suspended for a week without pay. Am I understood?

"Yes, Captain."

"Yes sir," Rydon complied. "Let's go, Sergeant, get the gloves. We're taking it outside," he barked, stretching his arms and neck.

Columbia, South Carolina

400th Block of Westshore

8:34 p.m. Eastern Standard Time

1968 March 18, Monday

Having finished his traveling for the case, Rydon could finally give his undivided attention to the needs of his latest mission. Without an end in sight, the community was still divided without a justified reason. Politicians swept issues under the rug, police cover-ups were at an all-time high, and Rydon was losing his composure in chunks like a chisel on stone.

Gathering evidence, witness statements, Gabriella's notes, and his own reports, Rydon was able to see an escape route. Unaware of how long it would take to close the case, he at least had something to show for weeks of hard work.

"Hello?" Rydon answered the phone midsleep.

"Officer Toussaint, we need all officers to report to the station by 10 p.m."

"It's Monday. I only work nights on Thursdays, Lieutenant."

"Then pretend it's Thursday. We need our best at the station by ten o'clock, Officer Toussaint. Everyone at the station specifically named you as one of our finest."

"Thank you, Lieutenant, I appreciate it. What's going on at 10?" Rydon wondered, slowly waking from his nap.

"I can't say much over the phone, but we need you, Officer Toussaint. It's double pay if it means anything to you. I hope we can count on you."

"Yes sir, see you at ten."

Blythewood, South Carolina

Richland County Police Department

9:36 p.m. Eastern Standard Time

1968 March 18, Monday

Searching for a vacant spot in an overcrowded parking lot, Rydon left his car around the corner. Walking the rest of the way to the police station, something seemed odd about his current setting. The overcrowded parking lot didn't match the silence of the neighborhood.

"Officer Toussaint, glad you could make it. He's even early. I told you he was a keeper, Chief. Officer Toussaint, this is Vincent Lyles, our Chief of Police.

"Chief, this is Len Toussaint. One of the best rookies I've ever seen. He's been with us for a month now." Lieutenant Sampson said, introducing one of his favorites in true blue.

"Nice to meet you, Officer Toussaint, I've heard a lot about you. If you're as good as they say you are, I might have to watch my back before you take my job," Chief Lyles said full of dry humor.

"Thank you Chief, it's an honor to meet you," Rydon said, humbly.

"Did they tell you why you're here?" Chief Lyles wondered.

"Is it my promotion ceremony?"

"He's funny. I like this guy," Chief Lyles laughed, loud and slowly. "One day soon I'm sure," he said, slapping Rydon's arm as they shook hands. "We received an anonymous tip saying rioters from Orangeburg have been conspiring with citizens of Blythewood and Columbia to revolt tonight at eleven, all throughout Richland County.

"Word is they're coming in packs all around the city. We're going to have men stationed in different neighborhoods to resolve things before they get started," Chief Lyles said, explaining the game plan. "It's going to be a long night."

"I'm here to work, Chief, just let me know where you want me. I'm going to get some tea to wake me up a little and get dressed. I'll be ready to move at ten o'clock," Rydon surrendered his services, shaking hands before he left for the locker room.

Preparing for an all-out war, Rydon strapped on his bulletproof vest, laced his boots, and tightened the belt to his black and charcoal patterned army fatigue cargo pants.

69

After meeting the Chief of Police, Rydon felt at ease under what seemed like excellent leadership. The vibe he got from Chief Lyles was unmatched by anyone else he met during his stay in South Carolina.

Columbia, South Carolina

Richland County

1:43 a.m. Eastern Standard Time

1968 March 18, Tuesday

Roaming the streets for hours, there were no signs of disturbances, protestors, rioters, or looters anywhere in sight. Rydon and his platoon combed the silent streets of Richland County looking for trouble. Creeping into the early morning, the tipster not only embarrassed Captain Drew and Lieutenant Sampson in front of the Chief of Police but also wasted thousands of dollars in overtime work hours.

Making their rounds near Northshore and Westshore Road, Rydon couldn't help but recollect the events that took place just days earlier. Every location seemed to have a memory attached to it.

With the other platoons making their way to the last patrol location, they began to conference in the middle of the street before heading back to the station.

All of a sudden, the streets filled with people of the community like a basin of water, and the officers began to get a dose of their own medicine. They were completely surrounded by protestors in every direction. Megaphones overpowered the screams of the people and news cameras were there capturing every minute of footage.

We have you surrounded!

How does it feel being ambushed for no reason?!

Protect and serve, don't shoot to kill!

You're policemen! Not oppressors!

Citizens of Richland County and Orangeburg united like no other social demonstration noted in history. The policemen of Richland County were left befuddled. The looks on their faces ranged from embarrassed to ashamed.

A small pocket seemed impressed, pleasantly surprised even. A few disrespected, seeing the people as unappreciative and one in an ugly fury. Sergeant Lynch ordered his men to lock arms in a large semicircle, forcing the people to separate and leave the premises.

"This is a public disturbance. It's time to go home or you will be forcibly removed. In three minutes, we will have no choice but to take action."

No one moved a muscle but shouts from the protestors continued to pour in.

You can't hurt us more than you already have!

Do what you gotta do, oppressor!

You're the only one who disturbs the public around here!

You come to bring the pain, we come to bring peace!

As the crowd grew, it gained more and more momentum with people of all ages, ethnic groups, and backgrounds. Losing control of the situation, Sergeant Lynch acted swiftly. "We tried to warn you. You leave us with no other choice. Men, let's disburse this mob."

Moving hesitantly, the officers took their positions. "This is the last warning, in three seconds, we will have to deescalate this situation," Sergeant Lynch informed the crowd.

Don't waste your time, we're not moving!

"3..... 2..... 1....," Sergeant Lynch counted. "Men, it's time to take out the trash," Sergeant Lynch said in a muffled tone behind his face mask.

The word *trash* stung Rydon's eardrum like a hornet. He never heard a commanding officer refer to the city's most civil citizens as trash. Hanging his head in shame, Rydon proceeded toward a group of young men who seemed to be the rowdiest.

Resting his riot shield and armored gloves in the back seat of a nearby squad car, Rydon clapped his hands, holding up his fist as he lifted the glass of his face mask. "This is really impressive. Your point has been made but it's time to break this up fellas,"

"Now isn't the time for talking Officer T," David responded.

Full of attitude, Sergeant Lynch pushed the crowd of young men that Rydon was speaking to and forcibly hit an older gentleman with his nightstick, causing him to fall. A member of the crowd struck Sergeant Lynch with a punch to the side of the head, knocking him to the ground. While reaching for his can of tear gas, one of the youngsters kicked it out of his hand and jumped on him, having his way with the Sergeant.

After that, the riot had officially begun. Hundreds of people began attacking the men in blue from afar. Glass bottles, cans of paint, sticks, and rocks were hauled at the officers as they deflected them with their riot shields. Retaliating with tear gas, the officers sprayed the entire crowd, sparing no one.

Coming to his feet, Sergeant Lynch reached for his pistol as his next resort. Rydon placed his hand over Sergeant Lynch's and shook his head, hoping to change his mind.

"Let go of me, rookie!" Sergeant Lynch yanked away and ran off.

BANG!

Sergeant Lynch fired a round at the group of young men who attacked him. As the crowd scattered in a frenzy, he searched frantically for the person who had beaten him.

Rydon shielded his eyes from the tear gas in the air before closing his face mask. Looking for his partner, he hoped to avoid another cover-up. Through it all, he caught up to Sergeant Lynch who looked like a crazed animal, grabbing people in the crowd to take a look at their face.

In the shadows of the night, a figure walked toward Sergeant Lynch. Recognizing who the person was, Rydon took off in a full sprint toward the two.

News crews were the most dazed of them all – stuck in limbo between getting great coverage for a story or taking cover for their own safety. Interviews were taking place in the middle of arrests; many news teams fled the scene long ago. While others refused to leave no matter the circumstances.

The figure seemed to be approaching Sergeant Lynch as he aimed his pistol and prepared to fire another round. Diving from afar, Rydon tackled Sergeant Lynch as the gun went off.

Flying from his feet to the ground, Rydon body slammed Sergeant Lynch with his stomach pressed against his back, as they crashed to the pavement. Scuffling with his partner, Rydon removed the pistol from his hands by striking him in the ribs.

After securing handcuffs on Sergeant Lynch's wrists, Rydon threw him in the back of a paddy wagon with the looters and vandals who had been detained earlier in the night. As Rydon rushed to aid the figure in the dark, his world tumbled down before his eyes. "Gabby, Gabby say something!" Rydon cried out.

"Right on time, Officer Toussaint," she said, lying flat on the city street with her eyes still closed.

"You scared me, Peanut. I don't know what I would have done without you. I thought I told you to stay in my apartment and away from all of this. You're so hardheaded." Rydon said emotionally, wrapping his arms around her.

"People woke me up, knocking at your door. They invited me to a rally, not a riot," she said, still protecting her stomach.

"Come on lady, tell me all about it," Rydon said, vanishing into the night. Securing Gabriella into the front seat of a squad car, he forgot about his duty as an officer and focused on his job as a husband.

"Why were you laying down like that?" Rydon wondered.

"Like what?"

"A snow angel without snow."

"Relief. Man," she sighed. "You ever been shot at? Never mind," she frowned, releasing a stream of tears.

MAJC News 7: Live Report

Richland County

4:47 a.m. Eastern Standard Time

1968 March 18, Tuesday

After hours of mayhem, everything was finally back to normal. Aside from the picket signs on the ground, paint-stained streets, and shattered glass, the city was finally at peace.

The only sign of life came from the last remaining media member and their special guest. "Thank you, Lacey. Hi, I'm Evelyn Princeton live in Columbia after a rally turned riot left three people hospitalized and one policeman arrested.

I'm here with Officer Len Toussaint, a first-year officer with the Richland County Police Department. You looked like the boss the way you took control of the situation back there. How did you do it?"

"I wouldn't have been able to if it wasn't for the wisdom and advice from a really good friend of mine, my mentor Detective Dr. Rydon Tyme. He couldn't be with us every day here in Columbia. He was protesting with teachers in Florida, but his advice guided me through the process."

"Really, what did he tell you?" Evelyn said, instantly star struck.

"He told me to remain calm when everyone around me panics and to panic when everyone around me is calm. He also told me to monitor every situation during riots and act on the ones that posed the greatest threat."

"Dr. Tyme comes through once again even in his absence. Did he say anything else?" Evelyn wondered.

"Yes, he did actually. He told me if I ever saw you, to tell you that he loved watching you on the news."

"Did he really?" she said in shock.

"Yes, ma'am. He also told me to tell you that he wasn't dunking in Virginia the night you all aired the footage. He was actually right here in the Carolinas that night."

"Sorry, Dr. Tyme. Please forgive me and us," she stuttered, pleading to the camera. "Is he still here?" Evelyn hoped.

"Yes, ma'am. I spoke with him before we came this way tonight. Dr. Tyme is pretty low key, so you may have seen him and didn't even realize it."

75

"That man is such a mystery," she said, blushing into the camera. "Well, you learned from the best and it shows. We need more officers like you and the others here tonight who truly want to bring peace to our streets. I'm Evelyn Princeton, reporting live for MAJC News 7, back to you Lacey."

Washington, D.C

National Mall

9:13 a.m. Eastern Standard Time

1968 March 21, Friday

Hundreds of thousands of people gathered in front of the Washington monument awaiting Dr. Rydon Tyme's keynote address. The Peace in This Place rally was planned months earlier and came with perfect timing. Having witnessed the brutalities of the world first hand, Dr. Rydon Tyme sat patiently during his wife's time at the podium.

"Please ladies and gentlemen, give it up for our next speaker, Mrs. Gabriella Tyme."

"Thank you, Mr. Mayor, and thank you D.C.!" she screamed as the crowd cheered on. "Over the last month and a half, I've had the honor to live amongst the people of Durham and Chapel Hill, North Carolina; Macon, Georgia; Jacob City, Florida; and Columbia, South Carolina. One thing I noticed in every city was that they all shared the same struggle. That struggle was oppression," the mood of the crowd began to shift and people shouted praises, showing signs of agreement.

Tell 'em, girl!

"I will," Gabriella replied to the woman in the crowd, causing a ripple of light laughter. "Coming from up north and going to school in Michigan, I never faced the type of oppression as the people in each of those cities down south.

"Another commonality they all shared, no matter how bad things were, they all knew better days were coming. When I was in Macon, a little boy asked me a question that almost broke my heart," she paused, fighting back tears.

The audience gave a lengthy applause, allowing Gabriella to regain her composure. "I said I wasn't going to cry. Y'all saved me," she said as the crowd laughed. "But, the little boy asked why I was so happy all the time... I didn't know what he meant by that so I asked him to break it down for someone who wasn't as smart as him," she snickered, triggering a healthy laugh across the crowd.

"He said I was always *smiling and happy*, he couldn't understand why... I was still confused so I asked, *how should I be acting*?" Gabriella paused again as tears filled her eyes once more. He said, '*afraid, it's scary here.*'

77

"Our children are growing up in fear and if things don't change, that boy will become immune to his fears and will retaliate one day; what do you expect? it's human nature. Survival of the fittest, only the strong survive.

"No child should ever have to grow up in fear. I don't care what they look like," she shouted passionately.

Alright now.

Right!

"We have to end this war now. I want each of you to think of the last time you were scared, I mean truly afraid. Now think of who eased your pain. That little boy is still living in fear and the only person who can ease his pain is you. End this Civil Rights War now and bring peace to this place we call the United States of America!"

Barely able to maintain her composure at the end of her speech, Gabriella Tyme broke down, crying on the chest of her husband. In front of the world, Rydon consoled his wife as she stood beside him.

"She's right, people. She is absolutely right. No child should ever have to grow up in fear. Thank you, Mrs. Tyme. We really needed to hear that," the Mayor applauded.

"Next to the podium is a man who I've known for years. He's the only person I know who works as hard as the President of this great nation. Please, ladies and gentlemen, show your love for Dr. Rydon Tyme."

"Thank you, Mr. Mayor," Rydon paused, waving at the audience. "I appreciate you, brother," he said, talking over the cheers. "Please give another round of applause for Mrs. Gabriella Tyme.

"She had no idea what she signed up for when she traveled to those cities. This country has robbed her of her innocence over the last month and a half.

"It'd be nights I'd get home and tell her about my day and the first thing out her mouth was always, *No way, that's impossible.* Over the last six weeks, she saw what I meant with her own two eyes.

"She was in the middle of riots, rallies, and labor strikes. She was even shot at just a few days ago by police, my partner on the case. She later told me the only reason she walked his way was because she recognized his face."

That's a shame

"For my last case, I was assigned to join a police force in Richland County, South Carolina.

—

"There was a police shooting at South Carolina International University in February that prevented three students from attending their college graduation next month."

Wow

"Two were targeted, the third was hit by a stray bullet.

"I was hired to help determine if the commanding officer that day was true blue or just another rogue cop. I'm here to present my findings to you and the live audience watching on the Real Newz Network and other news stations around the world.

"What I found when I got to Columbia was that most of the cops there were great policemen. They followed orders, thought sensibly, and genuinely loved their jobs. The ring leader was my partner, Sergeant Christopher Lynch.

"Now, that's where things get tricky.

"Sergeant Lynch let generalizations cloud his view of an entire group of people. He insulted and harassed innocent citizens, profiled people in the neighborhood based on the way they looked. On top of it all, he was a shoot-first type of cop. I put my life on the line twice in one week because he let his itchy trigger finger get the best of him.

"This envelope, in my hand holds Sergeant Christopher Lynch's full police record. Over the last twenty years, he's shot at thirty-four suspects, wounding thirty."

Whaaat?

"He once told me that he doesn't miss a target. The man was proud of his record. There are people like this all over the country and if you all don't stand up and do something about it, things will *never* change, for the better at least," Rydon warned the audience in a stern, yet caring tone.

"Many of you may wonder, well, Dr. Tyme, what are you going to do about it? I'm glad you asked," he answered quickly as the crowd chuckled. "It's enough people in attendance today to take action, right now.

"We've prepared petitions that grant homeowners and renters the right to police their own neighborhoods. It will also require policemen to show their record to any citizen who requests it before, during, or after police harassment. We're defining harassment as not telling the suspect what they're suspected of before making physical contact.

"At the same time, we have to be responsible for our own actions. If you break the law, be prepared to face the consequences. But the only way they'll keep their hands off you is if you stand up for yourselves, right now."

True.

"Change some laws, so these young'ns out here watching and listening will grow up wanting to be politicians because of what you did, today! Not tomorrow... today!" Rydon shouted, pointing at the crowd.

Go ahead!

Right on.

Yes.

"Brother Cities: Detroit, and Highland Park... make some noise," Rydon said, acknowledging his home team. "Kalamazoo, West Michigan, Chicago, Indianapolis, West Coast, Down South, Midwest, East Coast, Where are you?!"

The crowd erupted from the front, back, to those standing in the Reflecting Pool. "There are children... six, seven, eight years old in those places, right now. Listening, watching ready to grow up and be president because of what we're doing today, not tomorrow, today!"

Today!

The audience echoed as Rydon wiped the sweat from his forehead, placing the black handkerchief back into his shirt pocket. "This law will be for your protection and it is not to be abused or we will be right back to square one over a different issue.

"This is what we asked for so men, it's time to step up and lace your boots. We need fifty men protecting every community from not just police who abuse the badge; but these women and children should feel safe when they go places, no matter what time it is, period! Because some folks have to work, bills don't pay themselves."

Thank you.

"Give these boys a role model or two, or three, or four, or five, you know?" Rydon spoke, letting his heart bleed pure emotion as the crowd applauded in response.

I know that's right.

"My wife left the stage a moment ago in tears because she yearns so much for change. We can do it together and it starts with you. We have to change ourselves, one person, at a time. Once we complete that mission, there will be peace in this place.

"Thank you," Rydon said, taking a step back to wave farewell.

"Ladies and gentlemen, give it up one more time for Detective Dr. Rydon Tyme!"

Rio de Janeiro, Brazil

Tyme Towers

4:13 Coordinated Universal Time

1968 November 7, Thursday

April 13, 1968

Dear Dr. Rydon Tyme,

I want to formally apologize for everything I put you through. I have a problem and I didn't know that until I sat in the back of that paddy wagon.

My goal when I got hired with the Richland County Police Department was to clean up the streets and to keep them that way. My first day on the job back in 1948, my partner and I made a routine traffic stop.

When I asked the man for his license and registration, he gave me nothing but trouble. I was intimidated. Scared is probably a better word. When I got back to the car to run his information, I couldn't stop my hands from shaking. I asked my commanding officer to finish the stop because I was too rattled to speak with any confidence.

He called me a "Rookie", got out of the car and told me to stand back and take notes. In those days, things were a lot worse than it is today. I remember him yelling at the man and eventually beating him up pretty bad, throwing him against his own car. I thought to myself, "Now that's power".

Ever since, I tried my best to live up to my Sergeant's expectations. Then I met you and realized my mentor didn't have power, he abused it. Watching you work, taught me what power really is. Power is respect. People respect you, they feared me.

What's really bad is it wasn't me that they feared. They feared the power that I abused. When I saw you calmly talking to those boys a few weeks ago, you were seconds away from controlling the situation the correct way. The way we learned at the academy. "Deescalate without force" they used to always say.

When I saw them getting ready to move and go on home, I stepped in, trying to steal your shine. As we both know things got pretty ugly. Please tell your wife I apologize with all my heart for taking a shot at her.

She and that strong lil fella were about the same height and I thought he was coming for me. Especially knowing I was looking for him. I was paranoid and thought my life was in danger. Not because of her but because of the many bad choices I made that night, Dr. Tyme.

I had no idea you were thee, Dr. Rydon Tyme. I'm a huge fan believe it or not. That's why I wrote you today. Happy birthday!

You are a great actor and master of disguise. Listen to me, I sound like the back of a book, I know, but you had me fooled. Never questioned Len Toussaint for one second.

I hope you and your wife can find it in your hearts to forgive me. I'll have a lot of time to reflect over the next few years. The judge sentenced me forty-eight months. I guess you reap what you sow, so I have no right to complain.

This is what I get for all the lives that I ruined over the last twenty years. I promise, when I get out, I will be rehabilitated and willing to do anything you need me to, to help bring peace to this place.

Respectfully yours,
Chris Lynch

"Make a Splash in the World"

www.LOTT48203.com

Prize Fighter

Preview

Highland Park, Michigan

15900 Woodward Avenue

5:55 a.m. Eastern Standard Time

1959 January 5, Monday

"You run like a cop. You've been undercover so long, you lost your swagger. Loosen up, Champ!" Marcel taunted, chucking an apple at Rydon.

"I run like a cop? That's a good thing, Marcel. Try finding one woman who says I don't look like the chosen one when I run and my badge flies through the wind," Rydon darted back, jogging next to Jo's pickup truck.

Marcel sat in the flatbed, throwing rotten fruit at Rydon, that he dodged or punched. Tosses came at various speeds, up and down Woodward Avenue.

"Champions don't have to run to impress the ladies. We just hold the belt and pose for the camera. The Chosen One, you were chosen... I like it. That's your new nickname, Champ," Marcel yelled, throwing a melon at Rydon's torso.

Marcel was the livewire of the crew. He and Rydon brought out the best in each other. During their training days at The Bag as amateur boxers, they were both top ten juniors in their weight classes.

The Bag was a historic Highland Park recreation center. Established in 1815 by four men: Toussaint Freeman, Wallace Goodson, Roy Shabazz, and Eli Tyme. The Bag groomed some of the greatest boxers in the history of the sport.

Flash Shabazz, Icy Isa, Raphael Ruh, Bernard "Bees" Beason, and The Masterful Marcel Riaz represented generations of champions who trained at The Bag. Boxers signed contracts as prize fighters that expired well beyond their days inside the four corners.

After retirement, prize fighters turned into recruiters. Searching for the next big thing to fill their void. Rydon turned down the Professional Boxing Association once in the past. Instead, he accepted a track and field scholarship at California Midwest University.

In the meantime, four of Rydon's Life or Liberty brothers went on to become light, middle, and heavyweight champions of the world. "Alright, Champ. Hit the bag for ten minutes then jump rope for ten minutes.

"Lift five sets of ten. We're working with one hundred and twenty-five pounds this week. We have to train your muscles first. Light work. After that, put another ten minutes on the speed bag, alternating hands and that's it for today."

Highland Park, Michigan

The Bag Recreation Center

8:05 a.m. Eastern Standard Time

1959 January 5, Monday

"Good day, not so old man. You're in better shape than I thought," Marcel boasted loudly, clapping his hands.

"I'm a Detective Marcel, we're always in shape," Rydon shrugged.

"We'll see. Let's go upstairs and talk about the contract."

Walking up the wooden structure of the two-story building, Rydon admired pictures, Championship Belts, Iron Fist Awards, newspaper clippings, ticket stubs, boxing trunks, gloves, shoes, mouthpieces, and tons of other memorabilia.

Rydon hadn't been back to the gym since he left for college at an early age. The familiar faces lining the walls enlightened him on what he missed in his absence. Lost in a trance inside a timeless capsule, Marcel brought him back to reality from the upstairs office.

"You'll make it up there with us," Marcel called out.

"Baby steps, Marcel. One day at a time," Rydon said, shadowboxing up the stairs.

"Good attitude! Hard work pays well. This is the contract we're offering you. It's a two-year deal because of your record as an amateur. It speaks for itself.

"The second year is what we call *The Boxer's Option*. Look it over and let me know what you think. I know you're a married man now so, go over it with the Mrs. and get it back to me by Friday, signed or not because its postdated on our end," Marcel said, handing Rydon the contract.

"I'm a grown man, Marcel. I can make decisions without my wife," Rydon, responded, skimming the pages.

"Even better!" Marcel clapped, pumping his fists. Read it over. Let me know if you have any questions. If not, we can get your licensing process started now."

—

Professional Boxing Association: Boxer's Option Premium

The Bag has been approved by the Professional Boxing Association's Board of Trustees and is thereby granted full authority to represent our brand. The Bag is authorized to offer employment to qualified amateur boxers on behalf of the Professional Boxing Association.

Section 1

Healthcare Act:

    a.   The Professional Boxing Association offers lifetime health care benefits to all boxers signed with the company.

Retirement Fund:

    a.   The Professional Boxing Association requires at least 5% of all earnings from professional bouts, to be paid into the boxer's Retirement Fund.

    b.   Retirement Funds can be disbursed in the following ways:

        1.   One large lump sum.

        2.   Monthly, weekly, or biweekly increments until funds have fully disbursed.

        3.   Endorsed to another.

    c.   All retired boxers are paid annual stipends worth 1% of their total career earnings.

    d.   2 tickets are reserved for all retired boxers wishing to attend Professional Boxing Association events. Reservations begin 24 hours before public sale and are subject to availability afterward.

    e.   2 tickets to the annual Boxer's Ball.

Section 2:

Terms of Agreement:

    a.   One season as defined by the Professional Boxing Association is equivalent to 10 fights during a 30-month span.

    b.   *Boxer's Option* guarantees the boxer up to 10 additional fights. So long as it lasts no longer than 30 months.

c. Any and all contract negotiations must be completed during the Professional Boxing Association off-season (July, August, and September).

d. All boxers are required to join the Boxer's Union.

Section 3:

Personal Conduct:

All boxers must entertain the media during press conferences at least once before and after (same day) prize fights.

a. Press conferences shall not last longer than 30 minutes unless the boxer consents.

b. Boxers are expected to act as law-abiding citizens. Misconduct will be handled on a case by case basis.

Section 4:

Compensation:

All purses are split 70/30. The event sponsor receives 70%.

I, Rydon Tyme, accept the terms of agreement as a prize fighter of the Professional Boxing Association.

x_____

Professional Boxer

x The Bag Recreation Center 1-9-1959

Witness

—

"You know what? I want Gabby to be with me when I sign it. I'll get it back to you by Friday," Rydon countered, scratching his head.

"Same ole, Don," Marcel laughed. "It's going to be good having everyone back in the gym again."

"Who's everyone?" Rydon wondered with peaked curiosity.

"Flash, Ruh, and Bees for sure. They're your sparring partners."

"Sparring partners? I haven't boxed live since I was thirteen. They're Champions. I need to warm up first. That's like walking with an antelope in the safari," Rydon warned.

"We have time, but we don't have time to waste. Warm-up fights would be useless for a person with your skill set," Marcel reminded him.

"I'll spar with the champs after sparing with your best boxers in the gym for a few days. I grew up sparring with Flash, Ruh, and Bees. I want to see what the young bucks are made of," Rydon reasoned.

"I'll tell you what, Ty Farmer is the real deal. He just needs some time," Marcel said, walking toward the window.

"How old is he?"

"Just turned twenty-one in November. He's got power. Fists are big as bricks and his hand-eye coordination is impeccable. If he lands a haymaker, you might retire a little early," Marcel informed him, watching his fighters train from the office window. "But, he's raw with two left feet and bad defense."

"If he has bad feet, I'd hit him twice before he throws a punch. Not to mention, landing a punch would mean I didn't see his punches coming. My eyes have gotten stronger over the years," Rydon gloated.

"Finally, you understand. Sparring with anyone besides polished boxers is a waste of time. On the other hand, Farmer could learn a lot from sparring with someone new. Speaking of which, this kid from Louisville stopped by yesterday. Said he's here for a week and wanted to know if he could train here.

"I don't mind loaning the gym to a traveler for a few days if he's serious about the craft, so I put him to the test. He beat my top three boxers in twenty-seven minutes – real time.

—

"Sixteen years old. Reminded me a lot of you but better. His trash talk was smoother than yours too. It was like poetry. That kid is going to be special. I told him to sign and date the gloves he used. They're hanging up over there," Marcel pointed to the wall. "He wrote, *I'm already the greatest of all times!* The kid knows he's bad," Marcel laughed.

"I hope he is better than me. I want to meet him. Did he whoop Farmer too?" Rydon wondered, gauging Farmer's skill set.

"I didn't let him fight Farmer. That could've gotten ugly, either way. I'll let you spar with the gym members over the weekend. After that, I'm throwing you to the wolves," Marcel said, breaking down the game plan.

"I wouldn't have it any other way. I just need to tune-up first," Rydon said, shadowboxing defensively.

"Any other concerns give me a call. The contract offer expires Friday, ninety-six hours is standard PBA protocol. They run a tight ship. Unfortunately, you can't box live without a contract, so get ready for a lot of cardio and weight training. See you tomorrow at five minutes to six."

"Good deal, peace," Rydon agreed in principle on his way out the door.

__Rydon Tyme: The Life of the Eye, Prize Fighter (3 of 5)__

—

L.O.T.T.

Leaders Of Tomorrow, Today

Michigan International University (2015)

Wake Up Little Lion (2016)

The Life of the Eye- Nobody Cares 5 of 5

Royal Comics Coming Soon…

ABOUT THE AUTHOR

Ali Muhammad was born and raised in Highland Park, Michigan. After graduating from Western Michigan University with a Bachelor of Science degree in Professional Education, Muhammad began his Teaching career in one of West Michigan's Title I public schools.

In 2015, Muhammad pursued a second career in writing and has four published works to date. Debut novel, *Michigan International University*. Children's book, *Wake Up Little Lion*, short stories: *Nobody Cares* and *Bad Move* from the *Rydon Tyme: Life of the Eye* series.

During production for LOTT Magazine (2018), Muhammad was promoted from Lead Writer to Editor-In-Chief. Bad Move is the final installment of a five-project production deal Muhammad signed with Leaders of Tomorrow, Today LLC in 2014.

www.ingramcontent.com/pod-product-compliance
Lightning Source LLC
Chambersburg PA
CBHW051923220626
47052CB00003B/557

*9 7 8 1 7 3 5 6 6 8 7 0 3 *